Displaced

Cristina Sanders

16pt

Read How You Want

LARGE PRINT BOOKS, BRAILLE & DAISY

Copyright Page from the Original Book

Displaced is the winner of the Storylines Tessa Duder Award for
Young Adult Fiction sponsored by Walker Books Australia.

First published in 2021
by Walker Books Australia Pty Ltd
Locked Bag 22, Newtown
NSW 2042 Australia
www.walkerbooks.com.au

The moral rights of the author have been asserted.

 A catalogue record for this
book is available from the
National Library of Australia

Typeset in Sorts Mill Goudy
Printed and bound in Australia by McPherson's Printing Group

10 9 8 7 6 5 4 3 2 1

COVER IMAGES: © mg7 / istock (girl);
© Robin Joyce / shutterstock (beach)

TABLE OF CONTENTS

CRISTINA SANDERS grew up in the family's Gateway Bookshop in Wellington, where all books were tested on children. She went on to work for some years in book marketing and publishing both in New Zealand and London, and has recently begun writing novels. Her book Jerningham, which is the story of the first colonial settlement of Wellington, was published in 2020. Displaced is her first young adult novel. Cristina lives in Hawke's Bay with her family, where she runs on the hills, and, whenever she can, sails away on tall ships.

www.cristinasanders.me

FOR ANDERS & ANNA TORINA LARSEN

AUTHOR'S NOTE

All characters in this book are fictional, other than Bror Friberg, the recruitment agent. Two of the first ships carrying Norwegian labourers to New Zealand were the *Ballarat* and the *Høvding* in 1872. Bror Friberg was on the *Høvding,* which also carried my family, the Larsens. The ship neither stopped for repairs in Cape Verde nor picked up a sailor. Both the *Balmoral* and the *Halfwellen* of this story are fictional, though some of the immigrant experiences are composites of many stories.

Place name spellings are the common use of the time. In some cases with hymns and psalms I have used the more modern New International Version (NIV) bible verses rather than the King James Version (KJV) to convey the sentiment more accurately.

CHAPTER ONE

South Atlantic Ocean, 1872

When Clem's body goes into the sea it falls fast, without hesitation, and is gone.

A sea burial is different to a burial on land. There is no digging. No man with his heavy shovel comes to remove the soil, to open a warm gap in the earth for a final bed. There is no slow lowering of a coffin and there is not the waiting, the waiting, the waiting for the first toss of earth as the mourners wonder, is it really so?

When Clem goes into the sea there is hardly a splash, and the box disappears instantly. There is no pause and no soil. The heavy chains at his feet pull him down and the scar on the water heals instantly. There is no way back.

Not for Clem.

Not for Eloise.

Eloise has passed the point of no return and Cornwall is behind her, on the other side of a wave below which

Clem still slips downwards, into the submarine depths of the South Atlantic. Eloise doesn't know for how long he falls, but there is a waiting of sorts on the deck while the ship's bell rings.

Maybe he is still falling.

Cornwall, September 1871

Eloise left the dusty road and followed Clem and Martha across the meadow.

Late afternoon sun slanted over the fields, hot on a countryside busy with harvest. Butterflies rose up from underfoot, disturbed by her skirts pulling through the grasses, fragile wings dancing against the gold. She held her arms out and drifted through the cloud. White yarrow and blue cornflowers ran in long swathes and late poppies were scattered like confetti. The field shimmered with insects, and a clean, dried-grass scent hung in the summer heat.

Clouds built in layers on the horizon, white on grey, the frisson of an approaching storm dragging the air, drawing shadows across the end of the balmy summer day.

Ahead, where the meadow ran into the wood, high up in an elm tree, was a fluttering. Starlings, thousands of them, gathered behind leaves on the verge of turning. The high branches bowed with the birds' weight and a sharp noise washed over the meadow: screeching and laughing in a distinctly starling cacophony.

A clutch of birds swooped out, small triangular wings tip to tip, flying low over the field, back to their perches. Another group followed, bursting from the branches, closely tucked with the same tight precision. They were building for something.

Clem stopped with his face up to the sun, Martha with him: two blond heads the colour of straw. Martha's bonnet hung by a tie from the back of her dress and Eloise pulled it free and handed it to her sister.

"If you lose another one, I can't protect you from Father again."

"Three hundred and twelve," said Martha, counting the birds on the wing, fast.

Clem dropped into the soft, yellow grass and leaned back on his elbows with his long legs stretched out. "It's a great trick, Martha," he said. "One of your many with no discernible use." He pulled on her skirt but she ignored him.

"Eighty-nine," she said, her eyes following another swarm overhead.

The squawking chatter increased as the birds surged out in a long, sinuous snake. They massed overhead, viscous and slippery against the dark blue sky. They flattened and floated, then flipped and towered, individual little birds sucked inside a rising column. At the top they poured out, rippling down like water, scattering in the fall.

Eloise watched, spellbound. The loose dots sucked back together to form a soft ball that wobbled across the sky – a pulsating ballet of wings. They fell out of the ball into a long silk scarf that shook and rippled along the fields before the whole mass tied itself in knots and broke apart, scattering on the ground.

And then, in a puff of wind, they blew like dust from one corner of the meadow to the other, folding over and over as they touched down.

"How extraordinary," said Clem, holding out his hand for Eloise to pull him up. His eyes were the blue of cornflowers at their best, just before they turned. The air thickened, promising thunder.

***

Through the bay window, the house lamps were already lit. Eloise chased Clem and Martha inside just as the rain began.

Billy stood by the window chewing the side of his thumb, and her mother walked about tapping her hand lightly on the furniture.

"Father told us to wait in here," Billy said. "Where's Matthew?"

Billy was twelve and growing haphazardly out of childhood, but under the bruised purple light pouring through the window he looked vulnerable and young. Billy, Martha and Clem were fair like their mother; Matthew and Eloise took their father's dark looks.

Past Billy and though the smear of glass, Matthew came into view bounding down the driveway. He had a switch in his hand and he waved it in the rain like a conductor directing a concert.

From the hallway, Eloise heard her father's voice reverberate through the darkening house. "Boy! Where have you been?"

"Walking, sir," Eloise heard Matthew say. "Just walking."

"I don't expect to be kept waiting by my own son. Inside with you!"

The door of the sitting room opened and Matthew ducked in, wet haired, his face guarded, the carefree smile lost. Robert Sansonnet followed, his tall frame changing the shape of the empty spaces in the room.

His eyes fell first on Martha, who stood awkwardly with raised shoulders and her mouth slightly open. Her eyes ran back and forwards along the skirting board, following an invisible, trapped mouse.

"Sit down, you half-witted rabbit. There! There's a chair. Sit in it, why won't you?"

Martha hesitated, blinking rapidly, her odd ways a beacon to Robert's anger. Clem guided her into a chair and perched on its arm. Eloise watched her father's tight face. He glared around the room at his wife and children, but his expression softened at Eloise. She was usually the one to have his favour.

"I've had a letter from your mother's brother," he said, speaking in a kinder voice, only to her.

Eloise had heard no mention of her uncle for years. There was a portrait of Uncle Horatio in the upstairs corridor, painted before he left for America. It hung on a dark wall, hidden away past paintings of the Cornish Coast and the farm. Eloise had always thought of Horatio as a pirate, a construct of the brightly oiled eyes that followed her, and the atmosphere of disquiet that came with his name, a whisper of one who had lived a life of unmentionable wrongdoing.

"Is he coming home?" Eloise asked.

Eloise felt her mother draw a long intake of breath and, turning, saw that her face was wet with quiet tears. Her mother was not a happy woman, but Eloise hadn't known her to cry. She had a slipping feeling, like she was falling slowly from her horse and there was nothing she could do but hold on.

"Horatio has sold the farm," said Robert. "Our home. The land, the buildings, everything. To an American." He spat out the word as if that was the worst of it, that their home should go to an American.

Heavy chains formed around Eloise's body and she fought to sit straight. Sickness dripped into her heart.

She belonged to this house, it framed her world. She had been born upstairs. She knew how the sun passed hourly through each windowpane and the smell of the garden in every season. Her growth was measured in lines behind the kitchen door and her treasures secreted in nooks in the walls and floors. Her feet had done their part in the rubbing of the wooden stairs, smooth and bowed slightly in the middle, and she knew their sound, the tune they played in the dry weather, creaking with the squeal of a prodded pig on the fourth and eighth. They had done so for generations.

"What about us?" Clem asked. "Where are we to go?"

Robert's face shifted, his irritation turning sour. "Horatio has gone to New Zealand. He says there are opportunities in the colony – cheap land, good farming. Fast prosperity, for those prepared to work for it. He's buying a farm. I have three sons, I'll provide labour."

None of his three sons smiled.

"I don't understand what you are saying, Father," said Matthew. He nearly matched his father in height, but was young-shouldered and narrow-hipped, still growing into his frame. "We're to join him in New Zealand?"

The telltale twitch in her father's jaw was cold water down Eloise's back. *Stop, Matthew,* she willed. Her brother was twenty, a man stepping out from behind his father's shadow. *Don't challenge him,* she pleaded soundlessly. But Matthew didn't look at her.

"You are suggesting we emigrate? Become farmers in the colonies?" There was an assertiveness in his voice that Eloise hadn't heard before.

"Don't you raise your voice to me. I am not suggesting anything. I am telling you. That is exactly what we will do. The farm is sold, we need to be gone by May and I intend to book passage tomorrow."

Matthew's shoulders squared and his chest lifted. Eloise held her breath, fearing a confrontation.

"You cannot dictate to us like this! Uproot us with no consultation, no discussion!"

"Boy—"

"I won't go to New Zealand!"

"Won't go? Won't go?" Robert took a step towards his son, who stood defiantly straight. "Who are you, boy, to tell me what this family will and won't do? There is nothing for you here. Your inheritance is at the grace of your uncle and if he says you will go to New Zealand and farm for it, that is what you will do."

"I will not!"

"Matthew!" cried Eloise. It was madness to talk back to their father. When the boys had been smaller he'd thrashed them for less.

The punch came fast, a heavy fist, the strength of it knocking Matthew to his knees. "You'll do as you're told."

Matthew raised his head, his face full of rage. For a horrible second Eloise thought he would leap up and attack his father but he stayed down, hand to his jaw, eyes flaring.

Robert Sansonnet dropped his shoulders, the anger gone out of him, diminished. "Go in for dinner, go on, all of you. Get up, boy, I didn't hurt you. No need for the show. Penelope, have a plate sent through to my study. You'll join me later. There is much to do."

The brutality of the punch dissolved into Eloise over the evening and through the night. It was a punch too strong for a boy and she saw how a father's violence could pass, with a fist, to his son. Even gentle Matthew might, in time, be driven to fight back. She knew it would always stay with her, the menace indelibly drawn, branded behind her eyes like a tattoo.

It hung there in her grief as the confusion became a reality. Piece by piece, furniture was sold, room after room was closed up, and the packing gained momentum.

***

Spring came with daffodils and the vivid green of sprouting grass. Eloise's childhood disappeared into crates and boxes, destined for the market or the poor house. The contents of the attic, which had lain undisturbed for generations, were handled without ceremony before being placed in this pile, or that. The family crib had sat in the hallway for a week before Penelope returned it to the attic. "It belongs to the house," she told Eloise.

Matthew was seldom at home. Over winter he had grown scarce, aloof from the family, often moody and irritable. Sometimes, surprisingly, Eloise caught him gazing out the window with a face full of softness and a silly smile so unlike his usual lively expression.

Clem and Eloise were sent around the district, dispensing books to the school, clothing to the poor. One cold morning they walked out with clothes for the housekeeper's daughter, though Eloise wondered at the use of dancing shoes and fine gloves in a scullery. They passed through the wicket gate, blowing long breath-trumpets into the pale sky, their chatter a noisy babble like a stream over the cobbles. It was Clem who spotted Matthew disappearing over the stone wall to the neighbouring estate.

"Perhaps he's poaching rabbits," Clem said. "Selling them. Saving up so he can abandon us. He said he's not coming to New Zealand."

"That's absurd, Clem. Mr Montclair would shoot him. And of course he's coming to New Zealand." Though, when she said it, Eloise was not so sure. The new Matthew had become unreadable. "Perhaps he's visiting Rose?"

Clem laughed. "If he poaches Rose, Montclair will shoot him for sure."

It had been years since Eloise had seen their reclusive neighbours, other than at Christmas time when the grand family blessed the village and sat warmly muffled in their ancestral pew. There was bad blood between her father and Mr Montclair, though she didn't know the history. The idea of Matthew climbing the wall for a romantic tryst with the mysterious Rose was thrilling. She tugged at Clem's sleeve. "Let's look!" she said, but Clem wanted to get on. There was always something interesting on his horizon.

"Anyway," he said, extricating his sleeve from her hand, "Matthew would hardly be interested in Rose. She's just a child."

"She's the same age I am! Sixteen."

"Exactly. A darling child. Imagine if you had a beau! What fine entertainment that would be. Oh, I forgot. You do. Cousin Cornelius the chicken counter."

Eloise swung her bag at him and Clem skipped backwards. Cornelius was a distant cousin, a lonely, tongue-tied boy of Matthew's age, who visited every summer. Eloise neither liked nor disliked him, but he certainly wasn't her idea of a beau.

"Have you written to tell him you are sailing away?" Clem called, running ahead. "Have you broken his heart? Perhaps he's risen to counting pigs and Father will send for him."

"I don't know why you laugh about stock-counting, Clem. You'll be counting the pigs on Uncle Horatio's farm."

"When I am a landowner, I'll invite Cornelius to come and count my pigs. Sheep, too."

"Well, he has two hands. He can count your five pigs on one, and five sheep on the other."

Clem swung around and waited for her to catch up. He wagged his finger at her. "You underestimate me, little pea. I know you're sad to leave, Martha is frightened and it's dreadful for Mother, too, of course. But for me and Billy, this is our chance, don't you see? If we stay here and Matthew gets the farm I'll end up like Cornelius, just a stock agent, a working man. But in New Zealand land is cheap – they're practically giving it away. I'll have my own farm. We'll be colonial gentry."

Colonial gentry sounded no better than Cornish to Eloise, but she didn't have the heart to say so. Clem was off again, too fast for her, up and over the rise where walkers could look down over the estate wall.

Eloise looked down. She saw a movement in the trees.

In the orchard, a little dog trotted out onto a path.

It was a sweet thing, with long white hair that trailed in the mud and a floppy red bow tied around its neck. In a skipping run behind it appeared a girl, wrapped in a dark winter cloak with a fur cap covering her head. She was lean and graceful, light on her feet. "Clem, look," cried Eloise, but Clem was on ahead, swinging his bags and whistling.

In a second, the girl dipped back into the trees, out of sight. She looked to have stepped straight from a romantic novel, dancing along a ribbon of enchantment to meet a lover, a whispered vision. Eloise was sure it was Rose, running to meet Matthew. Why not? Rose was a Montclair, but Matthew was strong and tall and funny and kind and the handsomest young man in the county. Romance, for Eloise, had not yet materialised beyond the pages of Austen or Brontë, but she knew it transcended impediments: it leaped over conventions and broke feuds. Love scaled walls.

"I saw her!" Eloise ran after Clem. "I saw Rose running to meet Matthew!"

Clem was having none of it. "Eloise, my favourite little ninny. Give up your romantic dreams. Rose's grandfather was an earl. You mustn't go around saying she's meeting Matthew in the orchard. He's probably stealing apples and there'll be trouble enough for that."

But when they got home, there was no sign of Matthew. Eloise smiled.

She went down to the sheep yards to find Billy, but he was with a group of old farmers, picking over the flock with their clever hands and closed faces. Eloise saw her father at a distance, leaning heavily on a gate, his hand rubbing through his thick black hair. He gazed northward over the rolling hills towards the coast. She joined him, lifting one boot onto the gate, folding her hand over the top in the way he did, and looking out into the empty green.

"Ah, Princess." He smiled and reached out to stroke her hair. "You'll be feeling the way I do. Saying goodbye, one field at a time. It's a sad business."

He had a rich, deep voice. He'd told her stories, when she was young, of knights and dragons and adventures, stories he had patched together from remnants of legends. The boys never sat still to listen and Martha was a blank fish, but Eloise would crawl onto his lap in the deep armchair by the fire and put her ear against the rumbling voice in his broad chest.

"Clem says we'll be colonial gentry in New Zealand," she said.

"Of course we will. There'll be dancing and singing lessons again for you, and piano lessons for Billy. We'll have a gig. And I'm not sorry to leave; the farm's gone downhill. I've had the worst luck with the sheep these years, the old crook McDonald sold me those bad rams. And lost so much on the horses. I was cheated there, should have made a fortune."

Eloise hadn't heard him mention the horses since the animals were sold. The stables by the river were derelict now.

"Circumstances were against me," he said. "But we can start again in New Zealand."

Eloise didn't question her father. He was unlucky, with a string of unfortunate events that had undermined his success. She stood by him, companionably, while the shadows of high clouds scudded across fields empty of animals. They were more peaceful than they had been for a long while.

"Can I ask you something, Father?"

"Anything, Princess."

He looked older, but Eloise couldn't pinpoint what had changed. His straight jaw was always clean shaven, and there was just the beginning of a touch of grey in his side whiskers. His ferocious black eyebrows were the same, and the lines on his face were accumulating only slowly. Was he thinner in his clothes? There was a tiredness about his eyes. She was unused to seeing him defeated. She didn't know from where this talk of failure had come.

"Why are we forbidden from knowing the Montclairs? What did they do?"

Robert pushed away from the gate and stretched his back. With a tilt of his head he regarded Eloise, standing with her chin up, waiting for his answer. Eventually, he turned back to his pose overlooking the fields.

"It all happened a long time ago, Eloise. It is the reason your Uncle

Horatio can't come back to England. The Montclairs don't matter. We've managed to live on each side of that great wall for twenty-five years and now we are leaving, with never a word spoken. It's over."

"Matthew is in love with Rose."

As soon as she said it, she wished she hadn't. There was no immediate response but she felt a coldness in the day, although the sun still shone and no cloud passed over. She should, perhaps, have spoken to Matthew first. That he was in love explained his puzzling moods. Of course he would be morose to leave Rose behind. Could her father not see?

"How far has it gone?"

He sounded neither pleased nor angry.

"I don't know."

"Has he spoken to her father?"

"I don't know. I don't know anything. It might not be so."

There were starlings gathering in the trees but they stayed hidden. There was no glorious swooping dance across the fields when Eloise turned to go.

"Eloise." Her father caught her lightly by the elbow. "Not a word about this to anyone. Do you understand?"

"Yes, Father."

"That's a promise, then. Not a word."

She sensed something was wrong, but the days passed and nothing outwardly changed. Matthew still slipped away from them and wore his unapproachability firmly around his shoulders. Her father glowered over a silent table, his fists heavy on the cutlery.

In May they loaded the sea chests and said goodbye to the farm, with a constriction pulled so tightly around their lives that Eloise thought they would shatter.

They took the coach to Plymouth, and so to the docks.

CHAPTER TWO

They were five days out from Southampton, through the great swells of the English Channel and passing the Bay of Biscay, before Eloise found her sea feet. The journey had suffered a stormy start even before seasickness had drowned them all in wretched incapacity.

Robert had dragged Matthew aboard, so drunk or drugged he could not stand, his arms flailing until he fell into unconsciousness.

Eloise had been so sure Matthew had intended to remain behind. One by one, in the week before they left, he had taken them aside. To Eloise, his talk of looking after Mother and Martha was so obviously a goodbye.

And then on the docks, amid the tears and confusion of boarding, something had gone terribly wrong. When Matthew approached their mother, Eloise witnessed her father step between them, insisting he and Matthew bid farewell to England at a public house. An hour, he said, but they were gone all afternoon and came back on the turning tide, with Matthew incoherent. Robert carried him over his shoulder and dropped him in the boys' cabin. Eloise stood with her mother in the rain on the cold deck and watched the little rowboats pull the *Balmoral* out into the wind while Matthew lay unconscious below. Her father stood by, tight-lipped.

Now Matthew, like many passengers, barely left his cabin. There was no cure for seasickness other than water and rest, and no cure for the rift between Matthew and his father.

The barque ran south in the grip of a cold northerly blow, sails full with the malevolent force that ripped them away from England. Eloise felt the distance grow like a pulling away of her skin.

On deck she was light-headed, but without the lurching sickness that had laid her prone since leaving shore. She grasped the rail and stretched into the wind, blinking as the ship dived into a wave and watching the spume slap up the side, a spray of salt droplets cold on her face. She gripped tighter, feeling energy in the wood under her hands and the water on her cheek, stirred back to life by the pulse of the wake busting from the ship. It was better on deck than in the pocket of a cabin, which reeked of a week's nausea.

England's thin line of coast, long gone, was replaced by a sea-mist mirage. Everything Eloise had ever known had sunk below the horizon while her eyes were closed. Gone so fast. The farm, her friends, the countryside. Everything that made up the blood in her body. There was nothing now but an ocean of water, and she was the centre of the visible world.

Salt spindrifts beat a rhythm off the bowsprit and blew away along the deck.

Already they were so far out to sea it was impossible ever to return home.

She was surprised to see Martha come up on deck alone. With a blanket wrapped around her like a shawl, she moved awkwardly across the deck, a mix of the rolling surface and her normal loose-limbed gait. Of all of them, Martha was the least sickened by the ship's motion, but she was deeply affected in her spirit. She didn't like changes in her routine, she needed a steady world. She spent long hours in their cabin, her face closed to Eloise, tapping her fingers and flinching at the noises: the slap of the water and creaking of the ship, the banging of doors and the voices of the other passengers through the thin partitions, the calls of the sailors and, more distantly, the sound of the two hundred souls below deck and the animals that accompanied them.

In the corridor outside the cabins were crates of noisy birds, starlings that were being transported, as they were, for a new life in the colony. They should have been plump and shiny and flying through the sky, but had lost their sheen, and the stars on their plumage became dull in the sunless space. They were listless, caged slaves. Eloise hated their inside smell and clatter, but Martha stood in front of the cages for hours, studying them intently.

"Come and enjoy the cold with me, Martha," said Eloise as her sister pushed an old felt hat down over her undressed hair. Eloise held out her hand to catch her.

They walked unsteadily, linking arms and rolling with the swell, and leaned on the balustrade that separated the poop from the main deck.

Aching with tiredness and with her teeth chattering painfully in her icy face, Eloise looked out over the people below. Assisted passengers were divided into shifts on deck and it was family time. There were fair-haired children without caps or coats, skipping nimbly across ropes and running around the piled and lashed crates.

They were angelic, these children, their pale hair shining so brightly and moving so fast that Eloise's tired eyes couldn't keep up. They flew across the ship with halos of gold smeared out behind them and she gazed in bewilderment.

"They're Norwegians," said Martha. "Billy is going to teach them English hymns."

How extraordinary, thought Eloise. And how beautiful they look. She knew nothing about the emigrants on board, where they had come from or the circumstances that had put them here on this floating village. She'd heard of emigrants fleeing persecution or being drawn by promises of wealth. Were these Norwegians pushed or pulled? Eloise decided it must take both for people to leave their homes. No one would make such a trip without being both dragged and shoved.

***

Eloise found a niche on the upper deck hidden by a heavy roll of canvas from passers-by but with a clear view down to the deck below. The first mate, William Brown, brought her a blanket. She held a book, but although she had found her sea legs, reading made her nauseous, so she watched the sails overhead, marvelling at the hundreds of hues there were in an endlessly grey sea. She watched the lower deck passengers turn their faces to the wind, groups of women and children walking arm in arm. One woman might lean out, something on the water catching her eye or a friend in sight, and the group would bend and change direction, merging, breaking off, reforming.

Like her starlings in the meadow at home.

There were animals on deck, for the voyage and breeding stock for the farm, and the passengers saw to their care. Eloise watched as a girl was lifted high in the air by an older boy as Buttercup, the Sansonnets' hackney horse, put her nose out of the stall. Buttercup stood eighteen hands, with a shiny dun-coloured coat, white fetlocks and a white blaze on her lower nose, and a brown mane and tail. Their one remaining horse, after all the racing and breeding animals that had passed through her childhood. Eloise was pleased it was Buttercup who had earned the right to cross the world. She had been put to stallion a few weeks before they departed but they'd be months in the new country before they knew whether the horse was in foal. Buttercup blew a shuddering horsey breath on the child's hand and the girl squealed with delight, her arms wrapped around her brother's neck but her shining face fixed on the horse.

Matthew was deliberately elusive. For two weeks he had stayed closeted in the boys' cabin. Their mother had accepted he was suffering from prolonged seasickness. Robert, too, lingered and grew gaunt and grey. The cabin lad, Jack, brought Matthew his meals and Eloise left him alone. Of course he was sick, but it wasn't the sea.

As the winds grew consistent and the weather warmed, Matthew got up and disappeared down the companionway to the steerage quarters – against their father's strict instructions. There were a couple of London boys between decks and Matthew went where Eloise couldn't follow, loading victuals from his plate into a cloth to share with his new friends below.

Matthew had disowned her. Eloise wanted so much to talk to him, but there were no quiet places on the ship; there was no privacy. Had he really intended to stay behind? By telling her father about Rose had she unwittingly betrayed her brother? She felt sick at the thought. Surely not. She chewed her fingers and worried.

"Not a word to anyone," her father had made her promise. What had she done?

On the deck below, a group of little girls caught her eye. She had been following their movements without attention, like watching birds flitting across a landscape. Lively and spirited, they had white faces and long unbraided hair the pale gold of dried wheat. They ran around the deck, diving between the passengers, one crashing into a boy, who grabbed her, swung her around laughing and then dropped her back on deck to chase after her friends. Eloise observed the boy's graceful movements, his easy walk on the sloping deck. It was the same boy who had lifted his sister to pat Buttercup. His hair was thick and shining over a fine face. The girls collapsed in a heap at his feet and lay panting, entangled, looking up at him. Recuperating. And then one elbowed the others and they leaped up to race off again.

Eloise was enchanted by the girls. She made sure she was at her perch on the poop deck whenever it was family time below.

It was easy to agree when the minister's daughter asked her to help run a school for the children. Serenity Wix was only a couple of years older than Eloise, travelling with her father to a mission in Hawke's Bay. The minister was dull, but Eloise detected an interesting spark in Serenity.

She had already commandeered Billy for her school.

"It's something to do," Billy agreed later, when they were sitting in the girls' cabin after a heavy lunch, kicking their heels against the bunk boards and chatting. Billy swung his legs and fiddled with the fabric of Martha's dresses, which were piled high on her bed. Martha wasn't one for putting things away. Without the housekeeper to pick up after her, Martha's belongings lay where they fell, strewn across the tiny cabin. There were clothes and shoes piled on the bed and books all over the floor. Eloise shovelled the stuff into piles but made no further attempt to help her younger sister with her housekeeping.

"Serenity is bossier than you are," Billy added, pulling at a bonnet ribbon that had come loose and carelessly letting the stitches unravel, picking at the threads. "You'd think she was the preacher, not her father."

Eloise slapped his hand away from the clothes. "Leave it!" she said sharply. "Martha's as scruffy as a dog already without you pulling her clothes to bits."

"She's asked me to do singing lessons this afternoon," Billy said. "Serenity has. With the Norwegians. She said I have a lovely voice."

"Well, you do, Billy," said Eloise, messing his hair. "And lovely manners, and a lovely disposition and a lovely, high opinion of yourself."

She gave him a playful shove as the ship took a lurch over a swell and Billy toppled back on the bunk, tipping Martha's pile of stuff onto the floor.

"You should tidy that up," he told Eloise, but she just laughed and pinched his nose.

The door banged open and Martha stepped in. She was, indeed, dressed shabbily in an odd collection of a brown workday dress handed down from Eloise and still a size too big for her, wrapped with a pretty, but old, summer shawl of their mother's and a straw hat pulled firmly down over her pale hair, tied at the chin with a dirty ribbon. She took no notice of Billy on her bunk, and simply stepped over the mess on the floor. There was a box of books in the bunk's recess and she leaned past Billy to pull a volume out. She dropped it on the bed and pulled out another, before finding the one she was looking for. Then, still without a word, she waded through her dresses and back out the door, leaving it swinging open behind her.

"Hello, Martha!" called Billy, watching her bump against the wall of the passage with another roll of the ship.

She already had her head in the open book but did look back through the door with her fluttery blinking, as if startled to be addressed.

"Oh, hello." She held the book out. "I just ... you know..." She stood poised for a second, as if unsure where she or the sentence was going, and then gave one of her half-smiles, put out a hand to steady herself, and bumped off down the passageway.

***

Dinners on the *Balmoral* were served in the main saloon. It was a small compartment with a tiny fireplace, a central table with benches, and end cupboards. Down below, between decks, Clem said over two hundred people lived in one big communal space. They had no privacy other than a cloth curtain between the bunks, and some slept a whole family to a bed.

"You're not meant to go below," Eloise told him. "Captain says."

Clem shrugged her off. "Matthew's there," he said. He told her between decks was packed and cramped and smelt of cooking and damp clothes and rain came through the hatches. There was no fire. Eloise had no desire to descend to steerage class.

As they neared the equator and the temperature increased, her father wedged the saloon door open, the movement of the air providing some relief from the sticky heat. The Sansonnets dominated the space, the minister and Serenity took a corner. The only others in cabin class were a banker called Mr Duffy, his wife, their infant daughter and her nurse.

Mr Duffy was an amateur ornithologist and it was he who had brought the starlings in their cages.

Their scratching and clattering became a background noise to the voyage, but Eloise thought it a different sound to the birds in the trees. All the song notes were gone from their calls, and only their harsh voices remained.

Mr Duffy fed them and chattered to them and made notes of their health. He was bemused with Martha's obsessive study of their food intake and habits.

"Do you know," he told Eloise later, as they sat around the small dining table, "your sister can recognise each of the birds individually by its plumage? She's extraordinarily talented."

Robert, sitting across from him, guffawed.

"Why are you taking starlings to New Zealand?" asked Clem.

"The Acclimatisation Society has specifically requested them for the farms," said Mr Duffy. "Insects are ruining the crops. My starlings will eat the caterpillars."

"Don't New Zealand birds eat the caterpillars?"

"The native birds aren't much use. They live in the bush. No, good English birds will do the job best. And it will make the place feel more like home for all of us, don't you see, with starlings in the trees?"

As they journeyed south the air grew hotter, the birds lethargic and society on the *Balmoral* less formal. No one dressed for dinner. Robert, who had always insisted the family change for meals at home, came to the table in his day suit, as if the occasion warranted nothing more. There was plenty of food but it wasn't fresh; every mouthful was laden with grease and salt and the water tasted nasty, even in tea.

Robert chastised Clem for slouching forwards and rolling up his sleeves, and he slapped Billy for reaching across the table.

"They'll pick up their manners again when we arrive, I promise you," said her mother.

Eloise was proud that her mother made a polite effort to converse with the other passengers. Her father preferred not to engage. He was civil to the minister, Mr Wix, but rebuffed Mr Duffy's attempts to discuss business affairs.

"My wife's brother has our banking needs in hand. Good day to you, sir."

Matthew rarely ate with them. Eloise knew he was taking his meals straight from the galley and going below.

"The stuff they eat is pretty dreary," Clem told her. "Matthew took apples down yesterday and they thought it was Christmas."

"I don't like him going off down there," said Penelope. "He shouldn't be between decks at all, the captain told us that specifically. His place is here. Would you talk to him, Robert?"

Robert shook his head and continued with his dinner.

She looked at him quizzically. "Robert? Do you have any idea why he is so morose?"

"I do not," replied Robert.

Eloise saw a flush of displeasure in her father's face. Of course he knew what ailed Matthew, but like so many things, it was not a topic for discussion.

***

Eloise joined Serenity Wix and Billy on the main deck between the wide, sloping ladders to the poop. They made a school for the Norwegian children in the alcove, out of the wind.

Serenity's voice was clear. She used simple words, but Eloise heard poetry in the way she phrased her sentences, and liked her expressive tone. Eloise realised that, despite her austere appearance, Serenity was not at all dull. The little pupils sat cross-legged and listened attentively.

Clem leaned over the ladder railing where the emigrant boys were gathered. "Oh, miss! I know, miss!" he shouted, and thrust up his hand whenever Eloise asked a question.

"Please ask your brother to stop being a clown," Serenity told her, but it was hard to be angry with Clem.

Eloise smiled indulgently. "Yes, young man," she called out, pointing to Clem, and all the children swung around, laughing at Clem's cheeky expression.

"It's London, miss!" shouted Clem, and the boys around him cheered. "The capital city of England, miss. It's London!"

"Very good!" Eloise turned to her pupils, all pale skin and blue eyes in pretty, heart-shaped faces. "Now you say it: The capital city of England is London."

They sang the chorus of hymns, Serenity selecting examples with simple words and easy melodies, and Billy carried the tune.

"Be thou my vision, O Lord of my heart," they sang, their sweet voices lost in the vastness of the ocean all around.

"We can't hear you!" called Clem from the ladder.

"God will hear," said Serenity, and finally, at the end of the class, she allowed herself a little smile.

They were somewhere north of the equator, the *Balmoral* floating across gentle waters at a light clip, the sun bright and hot in a sky of the clearest blue, though there were clouds to the south predicting winds to come. Formalities had gone with the cool weather and the men had abandoned their jackets. Eloise, walking with Clem, had only a light cotton shawl to cover her bare arms, more to keep off the sun than for modesty.

She wiped away the moisture that gathered on her forehead and adjusted her straw hat. Clem took her arm as they walked, and they were steady, both at ease now, with the roll of the ship. They passed Martha and Serenity playing chess at the chart table, moving buttons in place of the pawns that had been lost overboard. Serenity was clearing the board, but Martha usually won their games. She had a good memory for previous strategies and was never beaten the same way twice.

They nodded to Captain McDonald standing at the wheel, and he nodded back. Mr Brown, the first mate, gave them a good morning and they exchanged some pleasantries with the ship's doctor, who declared that he was, after the first bout of seasickness, happily passing an uneventful journey.

A commotion down below drew them to the railings.

A strong sailor and two burly emigrants manhandled a shark onto the lower deck, dragging its muscular body from the sea. It thrashed about, impaled on one of the large boat hooks. A crowd gathered fast; there were screams and hollers and more people came running. Clem immediately rushed down to join the fray, and Billy and Matthew were there too, looking scruffy as labourers and jumping around the animal's slackening body. The cook despatched it with a long-bladed knife. Blood poured out over the scrubbed wood of the deck. The animals in their cages smelled the kill. Eloise heard the dogs barking in a frenzy and the horse, Buttercup, stomped and whinnied in her stall.

Fascinated, Eloise strained to get a better view as the cook split the shark, spilling its guts in a slippery tangle of entrails while a sailor dashed buckets of water over the carcass, splashing the passengers and pouring the mess over the side, the dark trail blossoming like ink in the sea below.

"They'll eat well tonight," said Mr Brown, nodding at the crowd. "Shark, with lemon and taters. That's a tasty soup and a fair change from salt pork and biscuits."

Soon after, there was another shout from high above in the crow's nest. For a while, in the excitement of the shark there was confusion, passengers slow to realise why the sailors leaped for the rigging and swarmed upwards.

It was Mr Brown, the first mate, who pointed aloft and the passengers turned their eyes to the top of the mainmast, where a small figure of a man leaned far out, shouting and waving his flag.

"It's a ship, that's what it is," said Mr Brown, "just come over the horizon!"

The shark was skinned, filleted and despatched to the galley before the oncoming ship was clearly visible to those on deck, a large four-masted barque cutting across their line from the west, moving slowly northwards in the light wind.

"She's the *Halfwellen* out of South Africa, on the slow haul to the West Indies, we're thinking," said Mr Brown. "And after that, she returns to England. Captain Wyndham is an old friend of our captain's. Here's a chance to send your letters home, in a roundabout way."

The ship's course veered slightly to port, and as they drew closer, again slightly more, and soon it appeared that the ships could run alongside. They hove to, and the ships bobbed on the ocean, close enough to see faces at the opposite rails.

Eloise stayed on deck and her mother rushed below to collect letters for the mailbag. Two, three boats were launched before she had gathered all her correspondence and sent it over to the *Halfwellen* for the journey back home. Letters to Cornelius and his mother, drawings from the girls of life on board to the housekeeper, instructions and advice to the American at the farm on the idiosyncrasies of the garden in the autumn. Heaven only knew when the next contact with the world would be.

Robert declined a visit over to the *Halfwellen,* choosing instead a lunch at Captain McDonald's table. He was seldom invited to the captain's quarters, and Eloise noticed this time he dressed carefully and formally. Of course, the boys were on an early boat across the divide.

"Can we go, Mother?" pleaded Eloise. "I'm sure to be allowed if you come with me. Can we?"

The visiting boats arrived, and a sprightly and clean-shaven Captain Wyndham was welcomed on board with a hearty hug by Captain McDonald, looking like a shaggy dog beside his taller and much slimmer old friend. They disappeared to the captain's quarters while lunch was prepared, and the ship's officers swapped stories.

"Don't interrupt the men," warned Penelope, but Eloise rushed up to Mr Brown to plead a trip across.

Mr Brown's companion, mate of the *Halfwellen,* smiled indulgently at her but shook his head. "We have no women on board to entertain you, young miss." He inclined his head to Penelope. "We have a party of explorers coming home from Africa, gentlemen all, but decidedly rough after two years in the interior."

He turned away from Eloise, but said in an aside to Penelope, "They've been away from any engagement with society for a long while, madam. Hardly congenial company for the young lady."

Penelope took her away, but Eloise spent the afternoon at the railings, longingly watching the boats come and go, her first view of something other than water and sky for weeks. They had passed close to the Cape Verde Islands but the view had been a disappointment. The passengers had stared out eagerly at a dark smudge in a rainy sky, far away in the distance; only the convergence of colourful birds had suggested that they were islands and not clouds on the horizon.

Today they'd had both a shark and a ship.

She was at the railings when the explorers came aboard. Their clothes were drab and they were thin and oddly mannered, one of them scratching his armpit constantly, twitching and slapping his shoulder, but to Eloise their faces were kind and intelligent and she longed to ask them where they had travelled and what they had seen. If she had been a man, she would have liked to have been an explorer.

Mid-afternoon the wind picked up. Mr Brown went three times to the captain, but still the men's voices were loud enough to hear across the deck, the tall Captain Wyndham a man of many stories and a great big laugh.

The passengers were ferried in the small boats back across a choppy sea and the explorers returned to their ship but still the captains dallied, eventually reappearing on deck as the swell slapped the sides of the boats. The growing winds pushed the ships together; Mr Brown had the crew standing by to set sail, fast.

Still they talked, and still Mr Brown waited at the top of the ladder to return Captain Wyndham over the divide. His men stood by anxiously, oars poised.

The *Balmoral* and the *Halfwellen* drifted closer.

With a final handshake and much back slapping, Captain Wyndham descended the ladder somewhat unsteadily and his mate scooped him aboard, settling behind his charge with hands firmly on his shoulders as the craft pushed off and the rowers dug in. Not the first time his mate has done that, Eloise thought.

By the time the small boat was halfway across, the *Balmoral*'s yards were braced, her jibs catching the wind, and the ship was gaining forward momentum, pulling away from the friendly *Halfwellen.*

Within half an hour they gathered a strong breeze from the nor'west and they were running fast due south. As darkness fell, the ships were many horizons apart.

The wind blew all night.

Eloise awoke to hear shutters banging and the groan of the timbers. Their door rattled and somewhere above there was a great flapping like an enormous bird taking off, beating giant wings on the ocean, unable to lift. She drifted in and out of dreams in her ship with laughing captains and sailors, and explorers with kind faces riding huge albatrosses over the water to Africa.

More banging and shouting. In her dream her mother came into her cabin, slapping on her bedding. Eloise pulled the pillow over her head and turned in her sleep.

In the morning she learned that Matthew was gone.

***

Eloise found her mother in the saloon, sobbing and pleading with the captain to turn the ship about and chase the *Halfwellen* up the Atlantic.

"Madam, we cannot catch her," he replied. He looked shaken, his upright stance abandoned as he sat at the table with Penelope's hands in his big paws. Robert stood downcast, leaning on the back of Penelope's chair, his head hanging.

"The winds that have blown all night have taken the *Halfwellen* far beyond our reach. Even if we had the speed to catch her, which we do not, we'd not find her out there on the ocean. It was truly remarkable that we crossed as we did."

"He may be drowned!" cried Penelope. "Oh! Why has no one seen him? Why did your men not bring him back?"

She clung to the captain, her eyes beseeching.

The door opened and Mr Brown stepped in, shaking his head in response to the captain's enquiring look.

"Look again!" cried Penelope. "Ask them! Everybody was on deck yesterday, watching the comings and goings. Someone will have seen him."

"Plenty saw him go over with your boys," said Mr Brown. "None remembers seeing him come back. We've searched the vessel, Captain. The boy's not aboard."

Robert turned to Clem and Billy, standing by with dropped heads.

"Clem. Once again. What did he say on the way over? Who did he talk to aboard? Where did he go?"

All heads turned to Clem, tousled and red eyed from a sleepless night, his face pinched as if in pain.

"There were lots of us in the longboat," said Clem quietly, his voice tight. He paused, chewing on his bottom lip. "Matthew was in front, Billy with me in the middle. He sat next to a sailor, but the mailbags were between them. I don't know if he talked to anyone. Billy?"

Billy started to cry and shook his head. It was his thirteenth birthday in two days and Matthew had promised to dangle him over the side of the ship as they crossed the equator. Billy had said he wanted to see the sharks close up. That was before they had caught one.

"He hasn't talked much for a while," Clem continued. "I haven't had a conversation with him all year about anything much. He's been below deck a lot of the trip–" the captain raised his eyebrows at this, "–playing cards with the London boys. That's where I thought he was when I went to bed. He doesn't usually come in until late."

"Did he talk to anyone on board the *Halfwellen?*" repeated Robert.

"Father, I don't know!" said Clem desperately. "Billy and I stayed with Mr Wix. The steward took us around and showed us the quarters and some of the collections – they had trays of stuffed birds and beetles pinned on boards. Then we played a game of quoits on deck with a sailor while the minister and the steward had tea. I don't know where Matthew went, he never took us along anywhere."

"And then, lad?" asked the captain.

"It started to blow. It picked up quickly and was quite fierce. You could feel it more on the *Halfwellen,* we were really rocking." His eyes closed. "The sailors were cussing."

"Why?"

"I don't know. Didn't like the way the boat was drifting, I suppose."

He stopped again until prodded by Robert. "Then the mate came out and starting pushing us back into the boats, fast. They were quite rough. Billy went first, the minister was with him in the front, they had baskets of fruit loaded in the boat so I couldn't fit. Mr Duffy called me in to see the birds."

"Birds?"

"In the galley. Live birds. Cages and cages of African birds. Mr Duffy wanted to swap some for his starlings but there wasn't time."

"You didn't think to ask where your brother was?" asked Penelope sharply.

"Billy went with the minister."

"Your *older* brother!" she screamed at him, rising out of her chair. "Where was *Matthew?*"

"I don't know!" Clem shouted back, tears now streaming down his face. "I didn't see him! I got shoved onto a boat, with Mr Duffy. Matthew wasn't on it. There was another in front of us. It was all rushed because the wind was picking up."

"Was he on it? The other boat? *Think!*"

"I don't know! There were big swells by then; half the time we couldn't see the ship!"

Penelope fell back into her chair then threw her face into her arms on the table, great sobs racking her body. Eloise put her arms around her, stroked her back, her tears falling too, into her mother's grey-streaked hair.

The captain stood up.

"Boys, get some rest. Duffy, Wix, Sansonnet. My cabin. Mr Brown, you too."

The men gone, Eloise and her mother sat with arms entwined and cried and cried. Martha sat close. She didn't cry, but twisted her handkerchief over and over in her hands.

CHAPTER THREE

They crossed the equator a few days after Matthew disappeared. In the saloon, the day passed without celebration. On deck the emigrant passengers threw a party and there was music and entertainment. Eloise heard it, but she stayed indoors with her mother.

Clem took Martha out to see the line, painted on Mr Brown's telescope to appear across the sea from horizon to horizon, but Penelope asked Robert to fetch them back. The minister, Mr Wix, had told her of the antics the sailors practised as a ship crossed the equator and she didn't want to lose another child, she said.

Robert told them on no account were they to leave the upper deck.

Eloise watched her father carefully, looking for some sign of guilt, an acknowledgement that he was at fault and had driven Matthew away. But Robert looked as bewildered as anyone. If he felt any guilt for his mistreatment of Matthew, it didn't show on his face.

Better the captain's explanation, that Matthew had fallen asleep on the *Halfwellen,* or been drunk with the sailors and not woken until the boat was far away. The captain and crew had all witnessed Matthew in a drunken state. Their opinion was clear.

Eloise knew they were wrong. Robert had dragged Matthew aboard against his will and Matthew had taken the first opportunity to get home. Back to Rose Montclair. The stupid, foolish, lovesick boy.

Dear God, thought Eloise. What have I done?

The *Balmoral* hit the doldrums and they lay for days with flagging sails on a flat, glassy sea. The still air was oppressive and they were motionless, stupefied in the heat. The girls made paper fans and lay awake at night, trying to stir the air in the tiny cabin.

The days came and went without forward momentum and everyone became tetchy. There was no reason why passengers on a becalmed ship should be any more lethargic than on one speeding along, but there it was. They stood irritably looking out at the wide, featureless sea. Mr Duffy's wife took pity on Eloise and lent her a collection of Jane Austen's books, but the romances made her cry.

Serenity and Billy continued the lessons for the Norwegian children, but Eloise excused herself, unable to concentrate.

She kept out of the sun and away from her parents, hidden in her cabin. Guilt lined her stomach like cold fish stew. She slept fitfully during the day and lay awake at night, as becalmed as the ship.

Finally, one night, Eloise felt a rocking in the small hours as the *Balmoral* creaked into motion again, gently stretching after a long time asleep.

She was wide awake.

"Martha?"

The was a quiet snuffle, but no movement.

Eloise lay still. The ship creaked again and returned to slumber.

She quietly climbed out of her bunk, wrapped a shawl around her nightdress, and slipped out of the cabin.

Outside, it was a brilliant night. A yellow moon high above the bow cast fragile shadows through the rigging, laying complicated lacework across the deck. Flashy stars and planets were scattered across the black velvet sky like chunky jewels, in colours she had never noticed in the night sky before: pinks and blues and even yellows, the sharp little points disappearing if she stared at them too intently. They were there below, too, where the sea should be, another black arena filled with stars. Barefoot, she crossed and went down to the lower deck, a strange compulsion drawing her close to the water.

Eloise leaned out over the rail and gazed down, eyes floating across the pricks of light that blazed their reflections back at her from deep down in the calm sea. If she leaped off the ship into the water she wasn't sure if she would fly or swim. After staring into the watery reflections, she started to see a light velvety glaze, a surface tension, close to the ship. But when she looked further out the reflection was pure, and at the horizon she couldn't tell where the sea ended and the sky began.

There was an eerie stillness in the world and she closed her eyes. Flying or floating, it made no difference. Matthew was still lost.

He could be awake this night too, on his ship, looking out into the cavern of stars, looking north towards England.

She found it hard to believe what he had done.

Was love really so powerful that her brother gave up everything? Eloise couldn't imagine a feeling so overwhelming. Rose must have bewitched him and Matthew lost all sense. Even without the wall between the families, a Sansonnet was no match for a Montclair. Did Matthew think he could rise dripping from the sea and Rose's father would shake him by the hand, happy to give his daughter to a homeless boy with no income?

The stupid, stupid fool.

Eloise felt such intense helplessness she was burned by it, in her throat and behind her eyes. The reflected stars were so clear, bright and sharp: intensely hot or freezing cold. She wasn't sure she'd be able to tell the difference, hot or cold, if she touched one. She might simply feel pain, as if there was no difference between hot and cold out there. There was no way to know how far the stars were below her in the water. She reached down with her hand, but the velvety surface trembled far out of her reach.

She stepped onto the lowest rail and leaned further.

"Hei, nei..." a voice, quiet, called from behind her.

***

She dropped back onto the deck and swung around.

Perched on a pile of sacks was one of the young Norwegian men, his summer straw hair luminous in the starlight. He was about Clem's age, with the same young stubble on his chin and square shoulders, an almost-man. The one who had lifted his sister to pat the horse. He had a hand raised anxiously, a twitch away from leaping to catch her should she climb the rails.

Eloise felt herself coming back from a far place. She registered the warm wood of the ship's deck under her bare feet and the hot moist air on her skin, as if she had been away somewhere, out of her body, fathoms down in the water with the stars.

She was confused, but not from fear or embarrassment.

The boy regarded her with a quizzical half-smile and Eloise saw kind eyes. She felt relieved, as if he had quietly rescued her, though she couldn't think from what. She had come out to see the stars and was glad to find another soul to bear witness to the magnificence of the night, under such a sky.

She held his eyes for a moment and then found it hard to look away.

Finally, she smiled, almost apologetically.

"Sorry," she whispered. "I spoiled–" she waved her hands at the sea, the sky. "This."

"Hello," he said, in two distinct notes, as if he sang the word.

Eloise turned back to the railing and after a minute the boy came and stood beside her, arms on the rail, looking out over the starlight caught in the calm sea. His sleeves were rolled up over firm arms, with strongly sculpted hands. It was intimate, to stand so close to a boy, she in her bare feet and nightdress, the night softly draped around them. The unreality of their surroundings and the distance from everywhere on earth left Eloise feeling adrift. This could be nothing untoward. Conventions, out here, didn't apply. There was simply nothing on which to tack them.

They were still for a while. Eloise watched for shooting stars, but they remained firmly attached to heaven.

"I'm Eloise," she said, and he smiled but didn't respond. She pointed to herself. "Eloise," she said slowly and then pointed to him. "What's your name?"

"Lars," he said, the r rolling. He pointed to himself. "Lars," and then to her, "Eloise."

He had a soft voice. He looked inquisitively at her, pointed to his eye as if crying and Eloise realised her face was wet with tears. Suddenly she was overcome with loss.

"It's my brother," she said. "My brother Matthew went over to the *Halfwellen* and didn't come back. We don't know what happened to him."

Lars mirrored her troubled face and nodded as if he understood. He raised his eyebrows for her to go on.

"I don't know whether he was trapped there somehow, or fell asleep, whether he stowed away, or maybe somehow on the crossing he fell off the boat and no one noticed. They had these big baskets of fruit, you see, that they were going to offload and they gave them to us instead. And we gave them barrels of something. I don't know, there were things going from ship to ship, gifts from the captains, I suppose, and the sea got choppy and no one was paying much attention to what was going on, they were so fast to get away in the end. We don't know what happened."

Lars looked out over the shining sea.

"You don't understand a word of all this do you?" asked Eloise. He smiled at her, recognising a question, and gave a slight shrug.

"Oh, but of course that's not it at all," she said. "I think Matthew was desperate to get back to England. He never wanted to come away at all. He's in love, you see, with a girl called Rose, who is well situated, and he has nothing to offer, and no matter what he makes of himself, her father will never allow it. It was all a dream, a lovely, romantic dream and he should have left it behind him. But he couldn't. He really was in love."

Lars nodded. She knew he was listening without understanding but it was so consoling to unburden herself to someone who heard the sounds without any knowledge behind the words. In talking to this Norwegian boy Eloise could voice her feelings without fear of judgement and without consequence. Because of his gentle face she told him about Martha, how odd she was, and getting odder now that she was out of her routine, and how they had never noticed when she was a girl but even Billy now saw that she couldn't look people in the eye or engage in conversation, and how embarrassing she was in the saloon when Mrs Duffy or the doctor tried to talk to her and she looked down at her shoes until they went away. Mrs Duffy asked if she was simple, but that wasn't it. Martha was so smart in some ways and so totally inadequate in others.

She told him about how Clem now had to step into Matthew's shoes and he was only eighteen, he was full of life and joy and would have to take on the older son responsibilities and have their father's heavy pressure on him, at least until Matthew came back. If he came back. If they ever saw him again.

She was back to Matthew. Everything always came back to Matthew.

She should have let him be. She should never have interfered, never spoken to her father.

She angrily plucked at the sleeve of her nightdress where a starling's feather had got stuck in the weave, but Lars reached out and gently stilled her pecking hand.

She looked down at his hand on hers for a moment.

Then he lifted his hand and pointed out to the horizon.

"Soloppgang," he said.

She raised her eyes.

There was a dark crimson line across the stars, a gash prising the sky from the sea, and the two of them stood together in wonder, watching as the dawn light poured in through the gap in the world's end.

***

Once free of the doldrums, the *Balmoral* flew quickly south, passing the Archipelago of Trinidade and Martin Vaz at night and on towards the coast of South America to pick up the Trades.

They spied another ship ahead and gave chase for over 100 miles, but lost her without contact. There was rain that kept them inside for days. Martha graduated to playing chess with the minister while Billy and Serenity learned two-part harmonies and sang hymns.

Penelope got up in the morning, slowly got dressed and joined them in the saloon where she sat, tired and sad, without talking, as day followed day and they pulled further and further away from Matthew.

Eloise went back to her teaching, Serenity to her preaching and Billy his music.

They had a rousing chorus on Sundays and the captain relaxed his rules and let the mixed choir onto the upper deck for the services.

Lars never came near the upper deck, but Eloise watched for him below and saw him everywhere. She sat in her nook as he ran around with his friends and held the jump-rope patiently for his little sisters. For a week he was assigned to Buttercup's stable, grooming the horse, feeding and petting her, tossing the soiled hay over the side.

Sometimes she came to the railing and he saw her. She would glance around carefully to check who was watching before she waved to him and he shot her a handsome smile back, tossing his long fair hair like a mane. She had scissors in her dressmaking bag. She thought what a pleasure it would be to wash and comb and cut his hair.

The weather grew cooler and school was cancelled more often than not. The captain was more relaxed, but wouldn't allow the steerage children into the saloon, or allow the girls and Billy below deck. Their school classes waited for fair weather.

One morning the wind was aft and the rain held off, and the children collected in their sheltered spot on deck. Eloise had the children reciting days of the week and then picking colours. She pointed to Billy's green cravat and, mostly, they shouted, "Green!"

"And this?" she said, pointing to the ladder rail.

"Black!"

"And this, the chair?"

"Brown!"

"The chair is brown."

"The chair is brown."

"The sky is blue."

"The sky is blue," in unison. Eloise was aware, out of the corner of her eye, of Lars's blond head behind her on the lower ladder. He was watching the lesson with a group of friends.

She thought she might teach him English, too.

"Anna, what colour is the sea?"

"The sea is blue."

"Thorina, what colour is my scarf?"

Thorina scratched her head. All the emigrants had lice. They itched and scratched for months on end.

"Pink," Eloise prompted her, suddenly and uncomfortably scratching her own neck where the collar rubbed. "My scarf is pink."

She gave up her position to Serenity, who settled the children down to read a story about a church mouse. Serenity spoke slowly and carefully and Eloise acted out the parts as she read. Her dancing, whiskery mouse had the children laughing.

Lars, graceful and angular, leaned over the ladder rail, watching her. Clem was beside him. The boys were chatting.

Eloise froze in her mouse pose, whiskers askew. The children laughed.

It wasn't Clem chatting and the Norwegian boy listening. Both boys were chatting. They were having a conversation. Lars spoke, and Clem replied. And Clem wasn't speaking Norwegian.

Lars caught her eye, suddenly aware of the mouse transfixed in his peripheral vision.

He shot her the same wry smile he'd worn the night under the stars, the smile he'd given her as he escorted her back to her cabin as the morning sun flooded the deck. The smile he'd worn as he had kissed her hand and said something charmingly foreign in his musical Norwegian.

She felt a blush sweep up her chest and bloom over her cheeks. She had spoken such a confession to this boy, assuming her secrets safe because he understood nothing. But it appeared he wasn't safe, or ignorant, at all.

Serenity's story went on: a bird came out of the sky. "A bird, please, Eloise!"

She became a bird, stretched out her wings and flew past the boys. "So you speak English?" she hissed at Lars, a firebrand bird.

Clem gave a start as she swept past. "I see you've met my sister!"

Lars put out his hand to stop her but she brushed him off and flew away. "Yes," he called to her back. "A little."

She continued on her path, flew away from the class, away from her brother and away from Lars, flew to her cabin and flung herself down on her bunk. But she found, as she pressed her hands to her burning cheeks, that she wasn't as embarrassed as she might have been. She was confused by the warmth she felt and told herself that it didn't matter. It wasn't as if the boy was one of her own, eavesdropping on her heart. He would go back down below.

***

The storm gave them plenty of warning, grey clouds collecting slowly on the horizon like thugs gathering for a fight. The air became shockingly electric and the winds buffeted one way and then backtracked the other, swirling around the *Balmoral* while the crew manoeuvred crates and barrels below and battened down the central hatches.

Robert had Lars strap Buttercup into her stall. Eloise watched from her perch. The horse sensed the changing pressure and jittered. She had lost some of her lustre and muscle but was in good health otherwise and, so far, travelling well. There was little to do but pad her stall with straw and lash the door. Lars was calm and efficient, did what was required for the animals and then went below, into the belly of the ship.

In the passengers' quarters, Jack the cabin lad was checking preparations. "No lamps," he said, moving from cabin to cabin, showing them how to strap into their beds for the duration. "And pack all this away," he said to Martha. "All these books and boards will be flying all over and knock you on the head. Strap the drawers. Tidy up, miss, ship-shape!"

Eloise helped her.

Clem and Billy worked with the minister to pack all loose items down and tie the cupboards closed in the saloon while Serenity sat with Mrs Duffy and her nurse, rocking the wailing baby. Mr Duffy checked his starlings, the cages roped tightly to uprights in the corridors. He covered them. There was nothing more he could do. They were restless on their perches, alert to the atmosphere.

The barometer dropped, the changing pressure palpable. Eloise said goodnight to her mother and tucked her in, but Penelope was glassy eyed and had disappeared with her loss into the tip and roll of the ship.

Above, the wind screamed in the rigging.

The storm hit. For three days it raged as the ship powered south, fuelled by giant engines. The family moved all together to the boys' cabin and huddled for comfort, holding fast to the storm straps, the sea thrashing against the portholes so heavily the girls were sure they would burst and the *Balmoral* be washed of all life, clean as a skeleton.

The noise smashed into their heads, day and night; the tin water pitchers fell and emptied and rattled across the floor. There was no sleep.

After the first night there were also no meals. They chewed on ships' biscuits and saw none of the crew – even the faithful Jack was commandeered away from their service. The sea surged up through the heads and flooded the cuddy, and there was a stench that pervaded the ship and sickened them as they crouched on the narrow bunks, nauseous and afraid.

Martha, always upset by the unknown, began a low keening. She sounded animal-like, her cry turning to a howl when the ship pitched high on the sea and the bow overstepped, crashing deep into a new trough. She seemed not to sleep at all, but quivered strangely. Even Penelope gave up trying to comfort her after two days of reassuring talk, and sat tired and impotent, exhausted by her inability to help any of her children. Eventually Martha's eyes glazed over, her howling stopped and she became unresponsive. She sat in the corner of the bunk, trying not to touch anyone, arms wrapped around her legs, tapping her fingers, rocking.

Slowly, the pitching subsided and sometime during the fourth night, the *Balmoral* drove clear of the storm.

***

Eloise disentangled herself from the wrecked cabin and followed her father, stepping over the debris in the saloon and out onto the almost righted deck. It was dawn, and the air was sharp and cold. All the sailors were labouring, the rigging was alive with men and the sails unfurling. She heard singing as ropes and crates and barrels were pulled out from down below and sails reworked and stitched on the deck.

The carpenter was shouting orders as he quickly managed a repair job on one of the hatches. The ship Eloise had imagined ripped to pieces and lying limp in the water was soon restored to health and she held fast to the railing, shaking and weak and astonished at the miracle.

"Do you see, Father? It's all right! I thought we were wrecked!"

The captain walked past, laughing.

"The roaring forties, Miss Sansonnet! We'll have more of those before we're through the Trades. Oh! But it's good to be moving along. Fresh air, what?"

Eloise breathed deeply, the salty air clear and sharp in her nostrils after the closed, damp odour of the cabin. She was debilitated with a pain in her stomach, hunger or thirst, and wanted comfort: warmth wrapped around her shoulders and hot food. For a moment, she was pathetically back in her childhood, running home from the cold fields to a crackling fire, hot broth and buttered scones on the table.

"Do you think we'll have hot dinner today, Father?"

Robert put his arm around her and rubbed her shoulder briskly. "I very much hope so! I never want to see one of those biscuits again. And I'd give my right arm for a tot of rum!"

Above the racket they heard a whinny and Eloise looked out for Lars below, but Buttercup was unpacked by an old man, who carefully stroked her down, cleaning away the straw.

"I should be seeing to the horse," said Robert. "Checking her over." But he stood flat on his feet, looking grey and tired. He turned away and went back inside, following the smell of bacon.

Serenity and Mr Wix were in the saloon, sweeping the floor.

Mr Duffy shuffled out of his cabin, head in his hands, moaning and shambolic. He had something sticky painted on the side of his beard and smelled of vomit. He went directly to the bird cages and started to unwrap the storm-cloths off them.

The first two cages had birds dead on the floor. Mr Duffy cried in rage. He ripped the coverings off all the cages and peered in with his wild, unfocused eyes at the stunned birds.

"Oh, my darlings! Oh, my lovelies!"

As Mr Duffy banged the cages in frustration there was a sudden flutter of wings; some of the birds, at least, reincarnated. Eloise felt a sharp relief at the squeaky chirp, the sound of life welcome.

Robert put his head out towards the galley and yelled for the boy to bring food, and then slumped at the table while the minister unlashed the furniture from under his feet.

"We'll see worse seas than that before we reach Napier, no doubt," said William Brown that evening, when the cabin passengers gathered unsteadily in the saloon and young Jack placed dinner plates on the table. A black eye covered half his cheek, and tender blue and red smashed skin painted his nose. The ship still ran at an angle with frequent lurches, and the pork occasionally slid across the table to join the dish of potatoes, but for the most part, after the wild ride through the storm, all was calm.

"It wasn't so bad now, lass," William Brown said to Martha, crouching down beside her as she sat slumped in her chair, eyes darting fast around the room, unable to settle. She was tapping her fingers on the underside of the table and counting under her breath. "We've run seas much higher than that in the *Balmoral* and never lost a sail. She's a good flyer, solid in a storm. Nothing to be frightened of. Though that was a long 'un to be sure; they don't usually run so high more than a day or so. Get some victuals in, girly, you'll be hungry."

Martha sat unmoving, but William Brown didn't notice and poured beer for the men, taking a tumbler for himself.

"There'll be dancing on the lower deck later," he said. "Always happens after a run like that. Makes you glad to be alive. You can go down and mingle. You lad," he pointed to Billy, "with your songs, you'll get a royal welcome. Oh yes, I've heard you! And you, young lassies, sure you'd like to dance after being cooped up for days?

It's quite respectable, ma'am, ship's tradition. Captain McDonald and the doctor will oversee proceedings, never seen them in such high spirits. It was a fierce one, but the *Balmoral* handles it. Solid in a storm," he repeated as he finished his beer and tripped out through the cabin door, "solid in a storm."

***

It was dark but not cold when they descended to the lower deck to join the celebrations. The music of fiddles and pipes was lively and loud. Eloise was surprised to be allowed down, but Penelope was calming Martha while their cabin was righted, and Robert remained alone at the table. Eloise thought he was too proud to go below and mingle with the emigrants, but reluctant to forbid them from attending an event presided over by the captain.

Eloise wore the simplest of her dresses, a pale blue two-tone cotton with a fitted jacket, and left on her study boots. She combed her hair and twisted it in a bunch tied with a life-affirming red ribbon. She wore no bonnet or hat; she had nothing simple to go with her dress and there was no one to advise her. Her etiquette lessons had not covered dancing with emigrants on a ship's deck after a storm.

She pinched her cheeks. *I will dance with only my brothers and Mrs Duffy,* she told her reflection in the glass, but her hand darted to the top drawer and she swiftly exchanged the cotton collar for a prettier one in lace.

They made an eccentric party; Serenity and her father in ministerial black, Mrs Duffy in a taffeta party dress and a fringed shawl. Her husband wore his dress coat but was shuffling and obviously unwell; young Jack tried to prop him up but was batted away. Behind them came their nurse in her day uniform, her arms for once free of the baby. Billy and Clem made no effort to dress, but looked dashing in their battered travelling suits. Eloise came at the back of the group and kept her eyes cast low as they descended the ladder, aware of the spectacle.

Lars would be there in the crowd. She wanted to see him, and didn't, in equal measure. She wanted to see the boy who had stood with her when the stars hung like gems in the black, before the sun tore the night apart so dramatically, and who had held her hand so gently. The boy without words who had heard her heart.

She shook her head to clear the nonsense and remind herself that boy was a Norwegian peasant. Labourers, Mr Duffy had told her, brought by the New Zealand Government to clear forests and build roads. Navvies and woodsmen, leaving terrible hardship in Norway. Poor as church mice, the lot of them.

Captain McDonald and the ship's doctor greeted them with a cheer amid the noise. The men were offered rum, which they all, including the minister, accepted gladly.

There was a huge crowd gathered in the spaces between the masts, around the crates. Eloise couldn't imagine how they lived below decks – families stowed like potatoes in a barrel. In the fray was a wild circle of dancers, the London boys whirling and clapping, young women too, lifting their dresses above their ankles and skipping on light feet.

There were guitars and flutes, and those with no instruments were making drums of whatever they could find, slapping the rhythm on the ship's bones.

"Come on, old stick!" shouted Clem to Eloise as he grabbed her waist and pulled her out onto the deck.

They twirled like drunks across the wooden boards, elbows and knees banging them at every turn, ducking between the dancers and swerving around the masts. Eloise was grateful for her boots; there were revellers coming at her from all directions. It felt wonderful to move again after so long in confinement. She unfurled her body, stretched out her cramped legs and pointed her toes.

"Isn't it the strangest thing!" shouted Clem in her ear. "A dancing boat in the middle of the ocean. Whatever do the fish make of this?" He laughed and swirled her again.

She stamped her feet and twirled around, her head tipping back to look up at the mast, which disappeared at the edge of the lamps' glow, their whole world, all these people, enclosed in this little circle of noise and light, a speck on the ocean.

A hand tugged her dress, and another, and she found herself encircled by her pupils, squeaking like mice at her and crashing with their arms out, pretending to be birds. "We're alive!" they seemed to cry. "We survived!"

Eloise chased them across the deck, catching them one by one and lifting them off the ground. Taking great gulps of the clear, fresh air, she felt vibrant and alive for the first time since Matthew had disappeared. They were far away from the sultry tropics now.

She put a child down and the little girl ran off, leaving Eloise tall and still, with her back against the railing, scanning the revellers for Lars's blond head. She would dance with him. He could laugh at her, her secrets and her confidences could spill over the deck like water, and she would still want to dance with him. Here, now, on this deck as they celebrated survival and even the captain had no rules, she could dance with him, the lovely Norwegian boy with the inquisitive eyes.

Her heart raced and she looked over the crowd as fair-haired dancers came in and out of the lamplight. But never him.

She waited, strung like a piano wire.

Billy came past with Serenity and they called to her but her eyes were burning now, looking for Lars.

Clem tried to pull her out among the dancers again but she slapped him away angrily.

"Where is he?" she asked desperately. "Your friend, the Norwegian boy, where is he?"

She heard her voice, shrill. It sounded like it belonged to someone else.

Clem was barely listening, calling over his shoulder to Billy, "I'm trying! She won't come!"

She held Clem by the shoulder. "Where is Lars?"

Clem looked bewildered. "Lars?"

She nodded, impatiently.

"You're waiting for Lars?"

"I'm not waiting for him!" She stamped her foot at how slow he was being; it was like speaking to a drunk man. He regarded her quizzically.

"Do you know where Lars is?" she repeated.

Clem shrugged. "Down below, I expect. Some of the Norwegians are sick."

"Sick?"

"Why are you asking about Lars, for heaven's sake? Come and dance with me!"

"Is Lars sick?"

"I don't know! Some of the little kids are. Probably not."

"Why isn't he here?"

"Has the storm made you crazy? What on earth's the matter with you?"

"Can you find out? Go and see if he is all right!"

"I can't hear you," he shouted over a roar of laughter nearby. He pulled her back into a gap on the port side rail. "You want me to go and see if that Norwegian boy, Lars, is sick? You want me to go below?"

"Yes. No. Yes, can you find out?"

"I'm not going down there. It stinks. It stunk to the heavens before the storm and now it's afloat with overflowing sewage. Why would I go below? What's got you rattled?"

"I need to know that he is all right. He ... he was looking after the horse. I wanted to thank him."

"Well, not now, you goose!" Clem was being pulled away by Billy, who was swinging past with a train of boys. He let himself be dragged into the melee but as he went he turned and shouted over his shoulder, pointing to a dark area by the mast.

"Look, there he is!"

And there he was. Leaning against the open hatch, half hidden below a tarpaulin, one foot on the step, poised on a threshold. His arms were folded against his chest. He was watching her.

Eloise felt the speed of the ship beneath her feet, aware that the space below her wasn't solid. She stared at him in the difficult light, and he back at her.

The train of dancers came through again and he disappeared behind them. When the path cleared he was gone.

"You are not dance," he said, and Eloise turned to find him standing next to her, almost at the exact spot where they had watched the sun rise over the equator. He wasn't the boy in her head at all; his cheeks were hollower and his shirt was grey and torn. There was blond stubble on his chin. For some reason in her mind she had transformed him into a gentleman in a fine white shirt, well fed and glossy. Here was his poor cousin.

"You speak English."

He smiled bashfully and the glossy picture she had built up in her mind faded and fell victim to the warm flesh and blood of him. The corners of his lips hooked upwards like a scroll.

"A little, yes. I am learning in London."

"You lived in London?"

"One year. I am working with railway, I am mechanic. In England everyone is speaking English."

His voice was musical with a strange rhythm and he was clear with his words, finishing them carefully. She asked him, "Why did you leave Norway?" and he tilted his head slightly as he regarded her. There was something obvious she hadn't understood.

"For work," he said. "But passage for New Zealand my father finds. For family all together. It is better."

Something compelled her to reach out her hand and touch his cheek. He started, but didn't pull away.

"Clem said you were sick."

"Me? No. But some sick, below."

"Your family?"

"My mother and my sister, Lenne. You are teaching English." His voice was like the bubbly waves of the ship's wake.

"Are they badly sick?"

"They get better. But the..." He made circular movements with his hands, and blowing noises.

"Storm?"

"The storm making more sick. But fever finish. Just sick."

"They had fever?"

He held his hands in a pinch. "Little. Now good."

His voice was slow and surprisingly deep, a man's voice, but soft, as if he had been speaking in enclosed spaces for too long. He used his hands neatly as he spoke, dividing his words into groups here and here.

"Have you been standing there for long? Watching me?"

He smiled. "Yes."

"Why don't you ask me to dance?"

"Why *do* I ask you?"

"No, why *don't* you ask me?"

"I don't."

"Not yet. But you should."

He was quite still, looking at her. She held his gaze.

"Miss..." he began, and she frowned.

"My name is Eloise."

"Yes," he replied. "I know. I remember."

There was a cough at her shoulder. Serenity stood there, looking stern.

"Would you come back in now, Eloise? My father and I are retiring and he asked me to fetch you."

Eloise threw a glance past Serenity. The lantern light shimmied over them, casting moving shadows, and Eloise knew she was almost invisible from the ladders. It was a chance. She reached for Serenity's hand.

"I'm going to dance," she said. "With my friend, Lars. Clem and Billy will chaperone. Please, Serenity. Tell your father I am with my brothers."

The older girl turned to Lars and held him with her serious expression. She had a preacher's way of opening the shutters to look behind a person's eyes. Lars's clear grey eyes didn't blink.

Almost imperceptibly, her hostility melted and she half-smiled, as if she had made an instant judgement of the man and the judgement was good. She gave a quick nod to Eloise and turned on her heel. Eloise took Lars's hand. His fingers were rough and dry, warm and soft all at the same time. She placed his other hand on her waist and he took her carefully, with amazement. As their eyes caught and held and they slipped into the tight stream of dancers on the deck, she felt as though there were some small but precious, intangible thing she couldn't understand that he gave to her, and she to him.

CHAPTER FOUR

New Zealand, August, 1872

Eloise sat on a trunk on the wharf surrounded by the crates and boxes of home. She had been watching and waiting for hours as unloading had gone around her, feeling land-sick on the uncertain ground. Her body was empty, her heart ripped out and left somewhere in the Southern Ocean.

Behind her, among a cluster of small coastal boats, lay the *Balmoral,* at rest now after her long voyage, showing no sign of the tragedies that had occurred within. Around midday, the captain crossed over to the agent's office with his heavy logbooks. He would report the safe arrival of all cargo and animals, and the loss of five lives, all fever cases, all buried at sea: two children, an elderly woman and a young man.

Billy and Martha lay on a pile of blankets, a nest made from stacked furniture. Martha stared at canoes on the pale lagoon while Billy looked skywards, his eyes open but seeing nothing. The big horse, Buttercup, was tied to the railing outside the hotel. She was rangy and lean, the shadow of her ribs etched on her sides and all the healthy glossiness gone from her. It was unlikely that she was with foal. How simple the prospect of a foal had seemed when they were still in Cornwall, and what an absurd gamble it appeared now they knew firsthand what such a journey entailed. But the horse, at least, was alive.

Matthew had disappeared and Clem had died, but the horse was alive. Was that true? Eloise sat in a stupor, holding onto her delirium to keep at bay the recurring day and nightmare of Clem in a box laid under the Jack, sliding down the plank off the ship with the chain weight at his feet pulling him straight down.

Her darling Clem.

Sucked into the sea.

How could such a thing have happened?

Napier's port, Ahuriri, lay on a tenuous earth barrier between the lagoon and the bay, and now at low tide its feet showed above sea level and the skirts of the wooden sheds trailed in the mud. Along the wharves, hatless men with rolled sleeves hauled freight and rolled barrels. Horses pulled heavily laden carts away into the back streets. A man came out of a side door of the hotel with a small hay box and a bucket of water for Buttercup, and the horse bent her head, blowing through her nostrils and slapping her lips in the pail.

Eloise was desperately thirsty. Neither her father nor mother was in sight, and the crew had gone into the hotel and not come back. She sat under a glaring sun, helpless and abandoned.

Eventually, she stood up slowly, rubbed her neck and looked around her. The dry land pitched like the sea.

A man in a suit stopped to look over their household jumble. He wore a black tie and a neatly trimmed moustache, and hope flickered quickly but fast died in Eloise. He was too young to be Uncle Horatio. Another man joined him, similarly dressed, this one much too old. They greeted each other warmly, shook hands and walked away. Eloise scanned the men passing by, looking for her uncle. Tall and dark like your father, her mother had told her. And elegant. Always well dressed.

Men passed up and down the wharf. None was tall, dark and elegant. She lay back down.

Later still, the slow clop of hooves tapped in her head. She woke more fully as she was lifted into a small cart and propped against their cabin trunks. She wrapped her arms around Martha and Billy. Next to her, brown-skinned men cleared the mountain of Sansonnet possessions off the wharf, easily lifting the heavy furniture onto a few large carts. They stacked the swaddled piano, dining room table and wooden crates, threw over a tarpaulin and tied it fast.

"Take it into storage," shouted her father, and carts rumbled by, men swung ropes.

Billy blinked in the harsh sunshine. There was nothing for him but light and shadows. The fever that had taken Clem had robbed Billy of his sight.

***

They were a week in a large, corner room on the first floor of the Commercial Hotel on Waghorn Street, a road back from the dock. Napier lay beyond, over the hill of Scinde Island that separated the port from the town. They had travelled over 15,000 miles across the world, but that last little hill was a mile too far.

There was a comfort of sorts, to be enclosed in the room. The transition from the ship's cabins to the wide, uncluttered spaces of the new land was too much to bear all at once. One window led out to the balcony and faced the twinkling blue of Hawke's Bay, but Eloise pulled the curtains against the sea. The other window looked over the stables towards the hill and she sat there, watching Buttercup slowly regain the strength in her legs. She wondered when she, too, would feel a desire to shake and stretch.

In front of the hotel was a holding area for cattle, roped-off beasts standing listlessly in the mud, and the noise and the stink permeated their days.

Eloise waited, confined, while her father went looking for her Uncle Horatio. Her mother had recovered from ship's fever, but other than as a physical presence, was absent in every conceivable way. She swallowed food that Eloise put in her mouth, but barely chewed. Occasionally she sat with a mouthful for too long, breathed and choked. Eloise resorted to scooping morsels out of her mother's mouth with her fingers and cutting them smaller, finally getting the titbits down with a mugful of beer.

Billy was lost and slept constantly. Eloise had to wake him to feed him soup and make him take a turn around the room. She imagined as he lay on his cot that he wasn't so much asleep as hiding behind closed eyelids, his blindness beyond understanding.

She tried to get him to walk outside but he grew angry and shook off her guiding arm.

"Eloise, I can't see! How can I go out if I can't see? There are lights and shadows but I'm underwater. Will I see again, Eloise? Am I to be blind forever?"

Eloise begged her father to arrange a doctor's visit and the hotel manager sent for Doctor Croft, who came over the hill from Napier the next day in a buggy.

He had no bag and no medicines and his examination involved nothing more than taking a pulse and staring intently at the patient while listening for irregular breathing.

For Penelope he prescribed hot food and bed rest. This was his cure for the pain of losing one son to a passing ship, burying a second at sea and having the world disappear for the third. Eat and rest.

Doctor Croft examined Billy but said there was no cure for his pitiable affliction and that once the fever had shut a body down so far as to render a child blind, it was sometimes kinder to let them go. Eloise asked him to leave.

The doctor was more interested in Martha, and tried to hold her hands as she tapped and steepled, tapped and steepled but Martha pulled away sharply from him and froze, and Eloise marched the doctor firmly to the door.

"Interesting case of nerves," he said as he backed out of the room.

There was nothing wrong with Martha. She was as healthy as the day they boarded.

Robert penned the animals, but soon had so many bidders for the pigs and the geese that he sold them all in a fit of pique, cursing Horatio for his absence. There was no record of Horatio at the wharves or in the town. No one matching his description had made enquiries after their vessel. There was no message left for the family with the shipping agents or at the post offices. Robert checked the records of land purchases, but there was no landowner Horatio Brooke in Napier or the surrounding areas.

One afternoon as Eloise stared out of the side window, she saw Mr Duffy coming up Waghorn Street. He stopped outside the Commercial. He was a familiar face after the week in limbo indoors and Eloise ran onto the balcony, leaned out and called down to him.

Mr Duffy pulled some envelopes from his breast pocket and waved them to her cheerily but by the time he had come upstairs her father had gone out onto the landing, closing the door firmly behind him.

Eloise watched the door and watched the road, and waited. Waiting had become a habit. For a girl brought up on the vast spaces of a Cornish farm she had turned into a chicken in a coop faster than she would ever have believed possible. Sadness hung like weights in her dresses, lumps in her body, heavy black patches in her soul. Lethargy claimed her and she didn't resist. Decisions were out of her hands. Eventually, Mr Duffy and her father walked into sight on the road and headed away together up Waghorn Street towards the hill and town, leaving no message or instructions.

The maid came to clean the room and tried, as she had every day, to get the family to come to the dining room for their evening meal, but Eloise again asked for trays to be brought up. Martha wasn't happy in new, noisy places, Billy wouldn't get out of bed and her mother could barely feed herself.

As the girl left, however, through the open door Eloise saw the light falling from somewhere out of sight onto the landing and she had a sudden urge to run down the stairs, out through the hotel and stand on firm ground in the daylight.

She called out to the maid, "I will come!"

The maid put her head back around the door. "Miss?"

"Set a place for me in the dining room. I will come down."

"Alone, miss?"

Eloise nodded curtly. Alone. Yes. She would look alone to the other diners. But in her head she would have Matthew with her, and Clem. And her friend Lars, too. She would invite Lars to the table with her brothers and he wouldn't be a peasant boy anymore but a gentleman, an equal. He would have clean clothes and smooth hands and her brothers would nudge and wink and say what a fine match he was for their sister, and they would eat a meal together at a table in a dining room that didn't roll and tumble and she wouldn't need to spoon-feed her mother or cut food for Billy.

She would pretend all this and then go for a walk, outside, in the fresh air.

And so she did.

***

She returned in the evening and the room was dim, the lamp unlit. There was no sign of her father. At least Martha hadn't been entirely hopeless. The dinner dishes were scattered messily across the table but they were empty, and Martha was walking Billy around the room, not paying much attention to where he put his feet. Eloise sat with her mother and took her hand, speaking quietly to her of the farmhouse in Cornwall and reminiscing about the animals and the landscape and the people they had left behind.

And so the evening passed, with small routines in a grey light.

The following day, late in the morning, Robert returned. He loaded Buttercup with their travel bags and few belongings.

There was no room to ride, so Robert had Penelope hold Buttercup's head and the girls led Billy between them. They were a sad group that walked away from the hotel, away from the sea.

Eloise stayed close to her mother, fearing that she would crumble, weak from the residue of the fever and months of inactivity. But Penelope held the horse firmly and put one foot in front of the other, movements learned long ago and more natural than anything that had come since. They made their dispirited way along the spit and over a causeway, stepping slowly and mechanically without looking around them. Billy asked where they were going, but Robert either didn't hear him or wouldn't reply. Their path took them upwards.

Halfway over the hill, Robert let them rest by the side of the road. They folded to the ground and looked back down to the harbour. There was another tall ship in the Iron Pot now, being refitted and reloaded, looking impossibly small to carry families and whole communities across the ocean. Eloise had seen it come in, working men and their families on the deck with the same bright countenance as Lars, gazing across the lagoon to the hills after months at sea. New Zealand was filling up with Scandinavian woodsmen.

Across the narrow road, blue-black birds with smart white bibs dipped their beaks in the spear-like flowers of flax.

They were glossy as starlings, but bigger, raw and energetic, the notes of their song punctuated with strange coughs and wheezes. They pecked aggressively. It seemed unlikely they would welcome Mr Duffy's scrawny starlings into their world.

Billy had his face turned up to the sun, eyes closed. His eyelids, almost transparently white, bulged with the fast movement of his pupils below, scanning the outdoor view of his imagination, turning towards the flap of a boat sail, the call of a gull, the clash of a passing horse's hooves on the stony road; things he would never see again.

"Have you found Uncle Horatio?" Billy's voice was sluggish, with a darkly submerged timbre that hadn't been there before the fever.

Robert didn't reply, seeming to have forgotten he had a son attached to the sad scarecrow of clothing dragging along with them.

Billy nudged Eloise. "You ask him," he said. "He'll answer you."

"Father?" asked Eloise. "Is there news of Uncle Horatio?"

"I have had a letter from him, yes. We just missed it in England. It followed us on the next ship, probably that one in the harbour there. It went to the bank and Duffy brought it to me."

Even Penelope turned her head at this.

"And? Are we going to our farm now?" asked Eloise.

"Ah, Princess," said Robert. His eyes were on some distant place, away across the harbour. "Your uncle hasn't bought a farm. Not yet. He is in a town called Thames, away north, and has some business opportunities there. I'm to go and meet him. I will leave you here, obviously. We'll set you up decently until I know what's to be done. You'll have to look after them Eloise, now, without the boys."

Billy turned his face away.

Eloise imagined that, in her father's eyes, they were all burdens.

"Now up you get and on we go," he said and pulled on the horse's bridle.

The road curved through a cutting in the hill and the horse and its hangers-on clopped over the top and began the descent back to the coast on the other side of the headland. Eloise could see now that it wasn't an island at all, but was attached to the far hills by tenuous snakes of land between the rivers.

Gulls cried harshly overhead and the smell of the sea didn't leave them. Once over the low saddle they could see down to a sparse town on the flat. Shakespeare Road, said the signpost, and Eloise thought Shakespeare would find beauty and tragedy enough here for several plays. But the comedy was lacking. And the love.

On this side, too, the blue Pacific shimmered brightly and dominated the view. There was no getting away from it. It was a different creature from Eloise's Cornish sea, where the horizon felt close and clouds thrashed the sky and the mood changed by the minute.

This was a wearingly cheerful ocean.

Along the coast, rolling breakers stretched away to far cliffs and spray billowed from the wave tops in a lacy mist, bright white as salt. A gravel spit curved from their perch to the distant hills and carried a long, straight limestone road, devoid of movement. The empty distance made Eloise feel desperately isolated. Napier didn't look like a town that would be easy to escape.

Inland were pockets of muddy scrub on the banks of a silvery, braided river. Between the river and the sea, Napier township was a bleak prospect, a collection of wooden houses and shops built on a grid of roads centred around a grand, two-storey stone building that looked like it had been dug out of an English town with a spade and dropped on the new ground, yet to be heeled in. "The Bank," said Robert. The whole place was raw and unpolished.

As they descended into the town, the view westward to the ranges opened up, the stacks of blue hills filed against the sky.

"Where are we?" asked Billy.

"Not far now, you don't need to stop and rest again, lad. Keep moving. I have arranged lodgings in town. You will be staying with the minister and his daughter."

"Serenity?" Martha asked in an unnatural, hopeful voice.

"I have just said so," replied her father. "Wix will be off soon to convert the heathen in some remote place, but the girl can stay with you until he calls for her."

"Where will Buttercup go?" asked Billy.

"There is stabling at the smithy. I'll hire something faster to take me to Thames."

They walked with the cart along the foot of the hill, through the edge of the town. Workers and shoppers stopped to watch the newcomers pass, but no one spoke to them, and Eloise saw no one of their own class. The road was dusty and the shops utilitarian and drab.

Robert led them through an open square and along a main road. They passed clusters of wooden cottages of various sizes with their backs to the hill, picket fences and porches to the road. One or two had front gardens and a homely appearance; others looked neglected. No two were alike. He stopped by a small, two-storey wooden villa with a covered verandah set back from the road.

"Here, Father?" asked Eloise, trying to keep the disappointment out of her voice. It was no better than any other house in the street.

A door flew open and Serenity came running out, her arms wide with affection. Eloise felt a strong warmth for the minister's daughter; her sensible face was a welcome sight. She wondered if Serenity could see the mire spread out all around them in a bleak aura. She had a dire need for friendship.

The afternoon sun struck the edge of the house and a tall, spiky cabbage tree in the lane cast striped shadows over the tin roof.

"Mr Duffy found it," Serenity said. "It's more spacious inside than it looks from the street. It was built for one of his clients, but he decided he wanted to be a country gentleman and so he moved to a farm."

"Whereas we have done the reverse: a farming family moved to town."

Robert unloaded their few possessions. With no hired help, Eloise and Martha carried the trunks inside while Billy stood on the porch, out of the way. They waited for an explanation. Who would look after them? For how long? When would Robert return? What should they do? But no explanations were given, and Eloise couldn't find a chink in her father's armour through which to pose a question.

Serenity, meanwhile, took Penelope into the back kitchen and made tea. Eloise found them in a peaceful setting; clean glass windows with white cotton curtains looking out to the overgrown plot, which stretched back to the cliff face. It was reassuringly simple. Her mother sat timidly in a painted wicker chair and Serenity covered her knees with a colourful knitted blanket. She took her shawl from her, folded it carefully and put it beside her, where Penelope's hand found it and stroked the raised pattern of the knit. Eloise watched the repetitive movement of her mother's hand, saw her vacant expression. She was with her sons out in the Atlantic, still.

"You've had your troubles," Serenity said to Eloise. "But your mother will come back, with love and faith. I have seen this before after such a loss." She took her friend's hand. "When Father comes home this evening, we will pray together, to bring her back to her family. You need her, and she must know that."

Robert left them to unpack and went down into the town to arrange for the furniture to be delivered and find a guide to take him to Thames. Home late in the evening, he called Eloise into the drawing room.

There were no chairs arranged, so Eloise sat on an upturned packing case and waited.

"I'm sorry to have to leave you here, with your mother so helpless. I count on you and Miss Wix between you to bring her around. I don't know how long I will be in Thames. I don't know what I can expect to find there. It's all most unsatisfactory. Horatio always was a selfish man, but this is inexcusable. Duffy at the Bank of New Zealand is in charge of my affairs, you can contact him if you need anything. There is an allowance for you. Serenity will cook and clean."

His expression was tender, but Eloise knew she was expected to understand and obey. Her father wasn't offering discussion.

"I have also received a letter from your mother's cousin, Cornelius Wainwright."

Cornelius! She felt a jolt at the mention of his name; a clutch of Cornwall in her heart. Cornelius didn't exist outside of the green hills of the farm, or summer trips to the sea. He belonged over the ocean, in a place where Clem was still alive and chasing her down a country lane.

"He seems to have drunk from the well of confidence since our departure and has written with a suggestion he would never have dared propose to my face. He has asked a specific question concerning you, Eloise."

"A question for me?"

"A question for me. Concerning you. A year ago I wouldn't have considered his suit. But God has sent us such trials. I left Cornwall with three strong sons to build our future and have arrived with none." He walked away from her, towards the window that faced the darkness of a foreign street. No one had come to shut the curtains. Her father tugged them closed.

The glow from the table lamp made dark pools beneath his eyebrows.

"I have accepted his proposal on your behalf, Eloise. He's an honest man, young and strong, and educated in farm work. He will join the family. You may consider yourself betrothed. I have informed your mother and she has no objection. I have told Cornelius to communicate with Duffy at the bank. I expect we shall see him within a year."

He left her in the simple room in the small house with the vast dark Napier night all around. She sat with her hands in her lap and her head bowed, but smiled as Clem's voice came clearly to her, shouting, "Cornelius the chicken counter!" with his laughter falling out of him like bubbles. She held Clem's presence as long as she could, and when he was gone she pictured Cornelius. He was a reliable man, steady, a part of their lives for as long back as she could remember, a life entwined with Clem and Matthew and Billy. He belonged to her other life:

before the terrible ocean divided her in two. Her father was right. A year ago she wouldn't have considered his suit either. But after all that had happened, having Cornelius here would, perhaps, hold them all together. The thought of wanting anything more seemed an extravagance.

***

Robert left the next day, riding inland into the bush with a native guide, up the trail to Taupo and on through the Waikato to Thames. There were ships that made the journey in better time, but Robert had determined never to step aboard a ship again, declaring he would rather face a hundred Māori warriors than another gut-wrenching bucket.

He left them in the care of Mr Wix, whose constant, piping voice called Eloise to see to her posture, her voice, her dress, to pick up after Martha, to set the table just so, to turn the brim of her bonnet down, be frugal with the water, make the tea weaker, look to your mother, look to your prayers. When the furniture arrived and Eloise arranged the drawing room as it had been at home, as much for her mother and Martha as for Billy, the minister said no, he preferred the dresser on the left, the chair by the window. He criticised their personal belongings as lavish and told Eloise to donate their surplus clothes and books to charity. He said the piano was too big and returned it to storage.

"Read your bible more slowly," he told her. "Read that passage again. And pause, Miss Sansonnet, on the word 'God'."

Eloise did everything he demanded, eternally obligated to Mr Wix for those days he had sat beside her brothers and mother as they burned with fever; for his nights in prayer as the ship flew past dark icebergs in the Southern Ocean and sleet clung to the sails. His will and perseverance brought both Billy and Penelope back when Eloise had thought them lost. It was Mr Wix who had closed Clem's eyes, who had arranged the carpenter to bring a coffin in which to lay her brother, whose words had been swallowed by the wind as they sent Clem to God.

Now they waited for the minister to be called to the mission at Waipukurau, a settlement thirty miles south, best known for horse racing and sheep shearing, a lonely outpost for a missionary. Serenity was to stay in Napier until the parish became better established, and for that Eloise was grateful.

Serenity had a simple faith that appealed to Eloise. She had a passion that had nothing to do with her father's fierce words and discipline, simply believing she was on earth to spread the word of God and that He said to be kind and good. Her faith was as honest and open-hearted as her father's was severe. Eloise envied her strong, unwavering belief that God was with her, always.

Serenity was patient with Martha, and reminded her to wash and brush her hair. She helped her lay her clothes out to make the morning dressing easier. Penelope also responded to her care and began to take care of herself again, like a diver surfacing from the depths. Eloise helped her mother clear a patch of garden and, with Martha, they planted the seeds from home in the soft soil of New Zealand.

Twice a week, Serenity and Mr Wix went to the immigrant barracks on the hill to preach to the Scandinavian women, who waited while their men established homes in the Seventy Mile Bush. Eloise imagined Lars swinging his axe in the sunshine alongside his father and brothers, building a strong wooden-framed house. People like Lars were always busy. They had occupations. They couldn't afford to sit and think; they were bees, building their lives around themselves.

In her empty hours, between petty, domestic tasks, Eloise thought of Lars and wondered if he had empty moments, and if he thought of her.

She went about her tasks with her wings clipped, far from her Cornish meadows. There were no wheat fields in Napier, no orchards. Living in a town there was no freedom, nowhere to run outside unobserved. She knew no one, and without older brothers or her father there were no introductions. The neighbours were tradespeople who worked in shops.

Without knowing what she was expected or allowed to do, she fell back on what she knew. She stayed caged inside, cared for her mother and Martha and Billy, sewed, gardened and rearranged the furniture.

It was Serenity who, with God's pass, could be careless of convention and explore this new world. And it was Serenity who brought news back to the family.

***

Serenity came running from the immigrants' barracks, her cheeks blushed with colour. She grabbed Eloise by the hand and pulled her out into the garden, insisting they walk a distance from the house.

"Oh, Eloise! I don't know how to tell you, I don't know what this means!"

Eloise pulled her friend to a stop and turned to face her. "Go on."

"There is news of Matthew!"

Her words hit Eloise like a rockfall. She staggered back, and Serenity steadied her as she crumpled against a stone wall, crouching in front of her, holding her arms.

"It was one of the elderly Norwegian men. He came on the *Høvding,* the ship that arrived after we did. He spoke of an English sailor who came aboard the *Høvding* when they stopped for repairs in Cape Verde, asking to work passage to New Zealand." She collected herself to make her words come calmly. "He said the man's name was Matthew and he was no sailor."

"We have to find him!" Eloise stood up.

"But wait, the story ends there. The man came ashore and went south with the Norwegians. Why would he do that?"

"He left?"

Serenity nodded. "He went to the camps in the bush with the *Høvding* men, following your friend Lars and their contingent."

Eloise's eyes narrowed. "What are you telling me?"

Serenity pushed her fingertips together, a subconscious prayer to help find a path, then said, "I don't know. I haven't had a chance to think, I ran straight back. Perhaps it wasn't your brother Matthew at all."

The tūī called in the flax, and the puffy clouds moved over the blue sky. Above on the cliff track they could hear a weka bird pushing around in the bush looking for worms, and perhaps Matthew had come back to them or perhaps it wasn't Matthew at all but another man, also called Matthew and also trying to get to New Zealand. Any of these things could be true.

They walked fast up the steep hill. Eloise, unused to the outdoors, was breathless.

The courtyard of the military barracks was an open square with a sod wall on one side facing long, low buildings. The militia had left at the end of the wars and the complex now received immigrants, processing and posting them to new beginnings. The Scandinavians had washed their clothes and regained their land legs and were healthy and bright. Flaxen-haired children ran around in the sharp sunshine of the yard, big leaping movements now with no boundaries to constrain them, making up for the time penned in at sea. Piles of round shot still remained in the square, discarded by the soldiers, and the children threw them against an iron tank where they struck with a pattering clang.

The women and elderly men stayed out of the sun, mending clothes, cooking on the communal stoves, exclaiming over the fresh meat and vegetables and milk for the children after the pitiful welfare at sea.

Eloise turned from one to the other, trying to get the story straight. Their translator, a Swede called Ana, understood Norwegian but her English was convoluted and slow.

"Where's my brother?" Eloise wanted to shout at them, but there was no straight answer. No one remembered details of the Englishman. He had worked his passage as a sailor. The Norwegians had little contact with him. The old man said some of the men mixed with the sailors but the man, Matthew, was young and aloof. He was medium height, maybe the same colouring as Eloise. He carried himself like a gentleman – for sure, he wasn't a sailor – he had an upright, military bearing, and had to learn his duties the hard way, from the others. He didn't speak Norwegian.

Eloise shot a glance at Serenity. It had to be Matthew.

"Medium height?"

Eloise didn't listen. "It has to be him!"

Before they left, Ana asked for a blessing and gathered the women together. Eloise stood impatiently to the side with her head bowed as Serenity blessed the women and elderly men and quoted from John 1:29. "Behold the Lamb of God, which taketh away the sin of the world."

Unadorned and clear, the words of the bible in Serenity's pure voice softened the edges of the barracks and tied the new settlers together.

The girls returned to the cottage unsure of what they knew and what to tell.

Penelope was in the kitchen. Eloise had left her the task of preparing a cabbage for vegetable stew, but she was standing with the cabbage in her hands, looking out the window. It was as if, when they weren't there to chivvy her along, she stopped existing.

Eloise took the vegetable from her hands and led her through to where Billy and Mr Wix waited. She sat her mother down and told them the news.

Animation flooded her mother's face. "I have to go and find him and bring him back," Penelope said immediately, getting up as if she meant to go straight to the stables and saddle the horse. "Pack me some food, and a blanket. Find me a guide, Mr Wix."

"Mother, we don't know if it is Matthew. Please don't get your hopes up."

"You can't go running down the road into the bush," the minister told Penelope. "Sit down now and be calm. I am going to Waipukurau in a few days, and I will send someone on to the camps to get news of him. If your son is there, I will send him back here."

"You are not good enough. He needs me. Why has he gone there? Did he stop and look for us here?"

Mr Wix bristled at this slight and Eloise shot him an apologetic look. "Mother, we can't know that it is Matthew. Mr Wix is right. You certainly cannot go on a journey in your fragile condition. Two weeks ago you could barely walk!"

No one had noticed Martha, who was standing in the doorway and looking at the floor, listening without contributing, like she always did, taking in everything or nothing. No one knew what Martha thought.

"We could go with the minister." They all turned to look at her. It was so unusual for Martha to speak out in a clear voice. "When the minister goes to his new parish, Eloise and I can go with him to find Matthew. Mother, you must stay here with Serenity and Billy. You know this is right."

They debated the options. It was clear that none of the women was prepared to wait for Robert to return, or to get a letter to him for advice. If it was Matthew — and they talked up all the reasons it could be and felt more and more certain as the discussion went on — they needed to find him urgently, before they lost him again.

Finally, it was agreed. Eloise and Martha would go together with Mr Wix and the convoy of Scandinavian women to the mission in Waipukurau. He would find them a guide to help search the bush camps for Matthew, where the Norwegians had settled. Norsewood.

Penelope was animated and nervous and stood by the window, looking out into the road and wringing her hands. Eloise wasn't sure this was an improvement on her previous stillness.

She held her mother's hands between her own and rubbed them, but Penelope wouldn't meet her eyes. "You need to look after Billy while we are gone," she said. "He will need you. You will look after him? We all need you, Mother. Will you promise?"

She nodded with quick jerks of her head.

When they found Matthew, he would know what to do. With her mother, with Billy, with her father. They could get on and buy a farm, build a house, settle down, find their way back from their broken state.

While Eloise packed bags for herself and Martha, Serenity suggested Penelope open her last chest from home, the one with her teacups and best china. The task brought Penelope back from the window and engaged her for the evening. She rearranged the plates and cups repeatedly, tutted over a chip in a plate and one cracked saucer, and placed pieces into Billy's hands for the boy to feel, to remind him of home. When Eloise and Martha left to find Matthew, Serenity had Penelope kneading bread, patiently, methodically.

Eloise kissed her and slipped away.

CHAPTER FIVE

South of Napier the land lay flat on wide grassy plains, hills rising bare, with ridges like fisted knuckles on either side. Along the straight road, recent rains had pushed vibrant green fern from the fertile soil of the verge and the sun chiselled bright lines on the edge of the foliage.

There were wading birds in the swamps, gangly things with thin legs that trailed as they flapped from the reeds into the air, and squat ducks escorting their tiny young onto the open water. Hawks circled overhead and the strange pūkeko ran across the landscape in a drunken dance – long-legged black and blue chickens.

As they went further inland the hills were less dramatic – smoother, with rounded tops devoid of trees. Scrub scratched up gullies, the ferns and spindly grey native plants giving way to thick grasses.

They passed plantings of Indian corn and fields of wheat, shimmering pale gold in the sun. Eloise thought of Lars and his uncombed blond hair. How at home he must be in this landscape, how he must blend into the hills! She let her thoughts stay with him, remembering the strength in his arms when he climbed the rigging, the rhythmic strong strokes with which he groomed the horse, his arm around her when they danced together after the storm. The way he had squeezed her waist and smiled, lips so close and then, reluctantly, had let her go. His restless grey eyes.

The land was so flat and fertile Eloise thought it was only a good Cornish plough away from productive farmstead. With her brothers, she could have been happy here.

The party went slowly, Eloise and Martha on Buttercup and Mr Wix on a sturdy pony purchased in the little town of Clive, on the way south of Napier. They travelled alongside the horse-drawn drays run by the wagoner, Mr McCreedy, which carried the Scandinavians' meagre possessions and a few weeks' supply of food. Mr McCreedy was a brash man, born in New Zealand to early traders, with a rough manner and crude talk. He drove one wagon; the other was operated by a lively young Māori man called Hemi.

Eloise had seen natives in town, and the women congregated in church in old-fashioned hats and strange assortments of clothes, but she had never spoken to one. The minister complimented Hemi on his surprisingly good command of English.

"Of course I speak English," Hemi told Mr Wix, lifting his chin to look down at the missionary. "I've been to school."

Hemi rode alongside the girls and told Eloise that Mr McCreedy was his father. He had a dark complexion and the wagoner was so flabby and pale she was unsure whether to believe him. The man bullied Hemi and called him rude names, but Hemi chuckled and got on with his work, perhaps thinking the abuse hid affection. If Mr McCreedy was his father he showed his love strangely. Eloise, lulled by the slow rocking of the horse, thought back to what she knew of fathers.

The Norwegians walked. Women, children and elderly men moved in procession along the limestone road, talking and singing with their heads high. They were a mix from both recent immigrant ships, nearly two hundred together. Eloise looked for the little girls, Lars's sisters, who had attended her lessons on the *Balmoral,* and saw them from time to time, walking with the women, sometimes riding on the cart. She caught glances from the women, but none spoke English, and Eloise saw their pity for her. The tragedy of her three brothers filled her up and she couldn't hold anyone's gaze.

The first night they stayed in the settlement of Te Aute. Some women were billeted in a local school and others in the hotel, camped in the bedrooms, lounge and bar. The minister was offered a room, but he gallantly gave it up to the elderly men of the party, to tent out with Mr McCreedy and Hemi. Eloise and Martha shared a bed with a young woman called Josephine while her mother, Anna, slept with two babies and three older girls on straw laid on the floor. Eloise was unsure quite where the babies belonged.

In the morning she noticed bug bites across Martha's face and she scratched at her neck, but her sister made no complaint. Martha was easy in the company of these strangers; there was no need to make small talk, no expectations or social norms. She was relaxed on horseback and sometimes walked the path alongside Hemi when he let the Norwegians drive. Hemi hardly talked to her, but occasionally distracted her with a whistle made from a blade of grass or a sudden handstand, which earned him a smile.

Eloise watched her sister's growing attachment to the Māori and his uncurbed way with her, but made no judgement. Martha, after all, was dressed haphazardly in a mismatched dress and jacket with thick socks showing over her boots, and her petticoat trailed with mud. She swung her arms as she walked, and didn't distance herself or discourage the man's antics. She did nothing to promote her elevated status among the peasant women. Perhaps it was an obvious error for the Māori man to confuse her with the labourers. Perhaps Eloise, too, was beginning to look like a peasant.

They got to Waipukurau late on Saturday night. The last miles they had doubled up on the horse, with one of the children – a young boy with a twisted ankle – perched up front. They were weary, and the hotel, when it came into view, was welcoming and large enough to accommodate them all inside or in the stables. Hemi, after seeing to Mr McCreedy's horses, took Buttercup out and brushed her down, ran his hands over her limbs and checked her hooves.

On Sunday they rested and Mr Wix gave a sermon to his new congregation in the front room of the hotel. This den, where the local run-holders gathered to drink and gamble in the evenings, was to be his church until money was approved for building. Surprisingly, he accepted this with equanimity.

Eloise wondered how low his expectations had been.

There was a midday dinner of mutton and potatoes, and for Eloise and Martha a chance to wash and change travel-soiled clothes in the afternoon.

Hemi was sent to deliver goods and mail to a station on the coastal hills and he returned in the evening with a milking cow and several chickens, a gift from the farmer for the minister in his new constituency.

Mr Wix decamped to his lodging, a wooden hut near the end of a long row on the south end of town with a small lean-to for his pony. The shack was sparsely furnished, with uneven wooden plank floors and canvas windows. There were two dingy bedrooms opening off a front living area. Cooking was done on the open hearth. There was one pot and a wooden pail for water from the river. Eloise pictured Serenity in this dark hovel and made a list in her head of items her friend would need when the time came, to take the edge off the bleakness.

The minister engaged a Māori woman to cook and clean. She introduced herself as Mary and said she was Hemi's mother, but when Eloise asked Hemi he laughed and said, "My mother? Okay, yes, sort of mother." The girls took the spare room for the night and Hemi brought them blankets and hot cakes with tea, and swept the bugs from the walls and floor. Long after they retired they heard his voice through the thin wall as he talked to Mary by the outside fire, their language strange and melodious, with frequent rumbles of soft laughter.

They left the minister the next morning, with his blessings and plenty of advice. "You're to find your brother and come straight back. Don't talk to the men or the wagoner. The boy, Hemi, can carry your messages. Don't let your sister uncover her head and don't travel on the Sabbath. Wear your gloves at all times. Don't slouch, Martha, God gave you a backbone the same as everyone else." As they backed away he seemed reluctant to let them go. He strode forward and took their hands, and they sang together the psalm for travellers:

I will lift up mine eyes unto the hills
from whence cometh my help?
My help cometh from the Lord,
who hath made heaven and earth.
The Lord himself is thy keeper–
They had to leave him standing there, his reedy voice soon lost in the

clatter of the horses and the shuffling of the travellers as they passed along the road.

They broke the journey next at Mr Fergusson's optimistically named Railway Hotel. There was no railway, and no sign of one, but the hotel was a substantial two-storey wooden building with a large barn on the outskirts of the little village of Takapau, at the end of the plains. There were plans, Mr McCreedy said, to bring a railway though.

Beyond, suddenly, was the forest, the start of the Seventy Mile Bush. It seemed an impenetrable barrier. In the afternoon light it appeared as a heavy black line drawn from the mountains across the valley and over the far hills. The forest ran all the way to the ocean.

Close up, Eloise saw layer upon layer of dense growth. There were ferns and supplejack in the undergrowth, pierced by broad-leafed palms and beeches with their small flickering leaves. Through them grew colossal giants, trees with girths that couldn't be circled by ten men. The forest came in a thousand different hues – all dark, and all green.

In the bush the light was gone; no sun reached through the canopy and down to the ground. Black stumps, ferns, mosses and rotting things littered the floor. The trees were bound together with a latticework of vines.

Where the forest darkness swallowed the road, a gatekeeper stood. It was the tallest tree Eloise had yet seen, with a mighty, mottled trunk that rose into the canopy and split into a bower. In its branches lived an entire jungle; climbers and mosses and ferns had taken root, small trees grew from pockets in the crumbling edifice of the mighty mother, a bird sheltering a whole world under its wings. Smaller trees leaned in with branches intertwined and curled and knotted together, so it was hard to see where one tree ended and another began.

"How can they possibly chop this down?" Eloise said to Martha.

"Who?"

"The Norwegians," said Eloise. "That's what they're here for. To clear this bush."

They looked around at the women, children and old men. They were tiny compared to the trees. Soft and fragile.

"I don't think so," said Martha.

***

The afternoon had been overcast and drizzling and the skies opened overnight with a hard downpour. The women lay packed together in a large room, restless, ears tuned to the rain striking the tin roof of Mr Fergusson's hotel like pelted pebbles, the wind picking a loose sheet and flapping it, a great bird trying to rise out of the mud.

Eloise lay on the floor, curled against her sister. She had never slept on the floor before. She was exhausted; the months of inactivity had not prepared her for such a journey. But as she lay awake on the hard boards she realised the physical pain had gone, the aches of the road washed in such tiredness that a hot bath could do no more. It was cathartic to lie there with these working women. By every reckoning she was as low as she had ever been, but she felt a spirit stirring.

Maybe tomorrow they would find Matthew.

When the party left in the morning on the last leg to Norsewood they were still tired, travel-dirty and worn, but the young women were loud as they sang and cheered their elders on. The drays could go no further and the goods were transferred to pack horses for the last miles through the bush, down a newly cleared dirt track to the Te Whiti clearing. A roadman went with them, guiding the horses past stumps and roots, laying manuka where the mud was deep and negotiating the small streams where boulders had been cleared and gravel laid to enable the horses to cross. Buttercup was a large horse on the track and Martha lay almost flat against her mane to avoid being decapitated by the low-hanging branches. At the streams Eloise, like the settler women, simply lifted her skirts and marched through the water without pausing. Her boots squelched with water and mud and pulled heavily on her legs.

In the forest it was quiet and oppressive. Eloise felt they passed in a bubble, all their clanking and rattling and the suck of the hooves on the path contained within their small sphere. Outside their breath, the bush hung like a still and heavy blanket. As they followed the track further into the bush her senses became numb; after days watching the mountains coming closer and closer she now couldn't feel them at all and was directionless. The conversations of the women ceased and Mr McCreedy's occasional outbursts of swearing as the horses stuck and sunk on the track became her point of reference as their march started and stopped, waited, and started again.

After an hour of walking she climbed up to join Martha on the horse, her arm around her sister's waist, her head on the younger girl's shoulder. The horse plodded on. She closed her eyes.

Eloise woke as she was lifted down from the horse. The sun was on her face and she felt open space and life around her again.

"Hei."

Under a dazzling blue sky in a clearing in the bush with the mountains towering behind, she stood against the horse, still half asleep, with Lars's arms around her. Her feet touched the ground but she didn't move away. The real Lars stood before her with earth beneath his feet and he was holding her. She had never stood with him before on solid ground and it felt miraculous. There was no better place to be. A smile started at the edge of his eyes and he carefully brushed a strand of hair back from her forehead.

"Hei, wake up, my friend," he said, and the smile pulled his high cheeks up as his eyes darted over her face.

"You are here." And they smiled at each other for so long in the wonder that it could be true, that they should be there, together, in a clearing in the bush when the chances of them standing and holding each other again had seemed infinitesimal.

Finally, he asked, "But why are you here?"

At that moment the women walkers arrived in the clearing and with them his mother and sisters, who came running for him. Lars scooped the little girls up in his arms and kissed them heartily and Hemi came to lead Buttercup away and unpack.

***

There was exhilaration in the meeting of the Norwegian men and their womenfolk, crying and laughter, scolding and hugs. The party had arrived earlier than expected and the men still came into the clearing from the bush, unshaven, dirty and tired, and they fell on their wives and children with relief.

There was no English sailor with the contingent that came forward. No Matthew.

Te Whiti was a bleak settlement. There was nothing but a tent from which a dishevelled English trader sold equipment, another tent that housed a butcher, and a crude wooden barracks, with loose planking and a rotting roof, strewn with bedding fern.

The men set to constructing rude shelters and lean-tos, hauling roughly cut branches across the grass for fast makeshift sheds over which they strung tarpaulins or thatched a Māori roof with the dense fronds of tree ferns.

Some men shouldered their bundles and walked away immediately into the bush with their wives and children close behind. Eloise was desperate at their departure before she could question them for news of her brother. She scanned the group for Lars but he had gone off with his axe, and the noise of felling came from the bush.

Lars's parents left for their section with the older boys, leaving their daughters in the barracks with Lars until there was a home for them, built somehow by magic out of the trees.

Eloise realised, perhaps at the same time as the truth dawned on the women, the great disappointment of their hopes. There was no grazing, no crops. The farms these families had come to were not farms at all. Their promised forty acres were squares of dense bush and giant trees marked out in the forest, all of which needed clearing, planting, building. There were surely years between a section of bush and a sustainable farm. She watched the collapse of dreams in the faces around her.

In the evening, when the men finally called a halt to their building, they cooked dinner over an open fire in the peaceful evening light, frying pans and pannikins perched on the embers. There was damper bread and a beef stew from provisions brought in from Waipukurau. Eloise wondered how long the provisions would last, and what would happen then.

When the shadows lengthened they piled more brushwood onto the fire to make it roar, a golden warm heart in the wilderness.

Eloise sat on the trampled earth with Lars, her back to a heavy totara log. Together they watched the flames dance along the wood, blue and green at the base with spitting sparks, white, orange and yellow at the tips, licking the branches and spilling upwards into the blue–black sky.

Across the fire, face bright in the flickering light, Martha played with a young boy and a piece of string, weaving it through his spread hands to create patterns. She was engrossed, and in the evening light her habitually pinched face was pretty and carefree.

How strange, thought Eloise, that things had been so difficult for Martha all her life, and here, in the dirt of a bush camp, she became herself.

Lars asked Eloise again why she had come and she told him about the story of the Englishman called Matthew, who fit Matthew's description, who had boarded the *Høvding* and followed them down the long sea route to New Zealand.

"You did not come here to find me?"

His voice was teasing, but she heard hope behind the question. She shook her head, sorry. She was sorry. She didn't have to tell him it couldn't be.

"Can you ask them for me? Someone may have seen him. Ask the passengers from the *Høvding?*"

He considered the faces in the firelight. After a while he stood up and walked across to a couple sitting away from the glow, a man and woman quietly talking. Eloise watched them, watched Lars as he gestured, making precise, clear movements with his expressive hands. The man appeared to frown, made some comments, shook his head. He pointed across the way. Lars moved around the group.

Martha joined her. "Has he found him?" she asked, as if it were as easy as that. As if Matthew were waiting out there in the bush to be found.

Eloise shook her head. "Not yet."

"You like Lars," she said.

There was Martha, surprising her again.

"That is observant of you."

Martha blinked rapidly and her expression was puzzled. Maybe there was smoke in her eyes or maybe she wanted to know more but didn't know how to ask. Eloise wouldn't help her; the feeling of being near Lars was not something she wanted to put into words.

Lars returned with a heavily bearded, intelligent-looking young man.

"Petta was on the *Høvding.* He remembers Matthew," Lars said.

Eloise stood up abruptly, her back suddenly cold without the log behind her, her face burning in the heat of the flames. Another huge log was thrown onto the fire and the sparks flared up, drawing a roar from the watchers.

"Ask him where he is!"

Lars asked Petta a simple question, and then translated the reply.

"He went to Dannevirke last week. To the Scandi camp."

"How far is it?"

Lars questioned the man again, but he shrugged and was hesitant in his reply.

"He doesn't know, Eloise. Maybe one day? Two? The man, the boss man, how do you say, the surveyor, go before with many men, all Denmark men from *Ballarat* ship, not *Høvding*. Matthew with them. It is a bad track. Slow. This is why we are bring here, to make this a road in the bush."

"But is it Matthew? Is it really Matthew?"

Lars was thoughtful and the men conversed for a long time, Lars pointing to his hair, the shape of his face. He motioned to Eloise and turned her towards the fire so the man could see her clearly.

Petta's face was hard to read in the flickering light. His eyebrows went up and down, he gave a nod and a shake, his hand out, about his shoulder height, shorter than Lars.

"Matthew is taller than you," Eloise interrupted and Lars brought his hand up, maybe this tall? And the other man shrugged again, his hand going up, turning over.

"Eloise. He thinks the man has brown hair. Not remember black hair and blue eye. Like you. Black hair and blue eye. I remember this. It is very, maybe you not say for a man ... so beautiful, this, together."

"What does he remember?"

"They play cards."

"Matthew plays cards!"

"He say young man, he think same old than me."

"Matthew is twenty."

"I am eighteen. Is possible. He has line on lip, perhaps." Petta nodded and he drew his nail to mark a scar on the upper lip. Eloise instinctively rubbed her own lip, rubbing the scar out. Matthew had no scar, not when she last saw him.

"He say Matthew has teeth not so good."

"What does that mean, not so good?"

Lars questioned the man again but, though he was eager to help, he was not forthcoming with anything positive. There were many settlers and many sailors on the ship. He didn't remember the details.

The girls laid a blanket on a dusty pallet on the floor in a corner of the barracks and washed as best they could using a handkerchief and warm water from their tin pot. They unlaced but otherwise lay down in their clothes. They spoke only briefly and for that Eloise was grateful, wanting to consider what they had learned. Why would Matthew keep going south? Did he think their new farm was down country? It was possible he had misinformation and had gone to look for them somewhere; there were English farms and stations dotted from Hawke's Bay and south of the forest towards Wellington.

There were men from the *Høvding* due into Te Whiti over the following days who might have more information, but Eloise didn't want to wait. If

Matthew was in the Dannevirke settlement, she would travel there.

She lay in the dark, with the shuffling of the women around her and the clicking of small things running across the roof. There were rats in the bush, Hemi said, big as your feet. You eat them when you're hungry, he told her, laughing. Chop off their tails and put them in the pot. Bush kai!

But it wasn't the rats keeping her awake. A short, brown-haired man with bad teeth and a scar on his upper lip, Petta had said. She remembered Matthew back home on the farm in Cornwall and her eyes stung as she held his picture in her mind. Tall and straight with strong shoulders and shiny black hair and a ready, clean smile. The Matthew who, back in England before the whole horrible trip had begun, before Clem had died and Billy gone blind, would slip away to meet Rose Montclair in the forbidden orchard.

For the first time since leaving Napier on her quest to find him, she felt doubt.

***

In the morning Lars left his sisters with the other children, called to work on the road by the foreman. Before he left he gave instructions to the young Norwegian, Josephine, that she was to question every man who came into the clearing for news of Matthew and report back to him in the evening.

"Do not leave!" Lars told Eloise as he shouldered his axe and spade and followed the men into the trees, disappearing from the clear morning light into the dark undergrowth in just a few paces.

Eloise questioned the storekeepers after they had set up their wares for the day. They didn't remember anyone speaking English.

"One looks the same as another," said Mr Sikes, the butcher, and he spat on the grass. "All tall and lean and strapping, with that serious way about them. Strong and wiry. Carrying huge loads on their backs and swinging their axes. And that's just the women!"

The men threw back their heads and roared with laughter. Sikes was missing several teeth.

"But do you remember a man among them who wasn't talking, as if he didn't speak their language?" she asked impatiently.

"Ah, they're talking all the time. But it's not English, little lady. Well, if it is, it's not like any English I've ever heard. You can't tell where one word ends and the other begins. All that blahdy blurdy gobbly gobbly they talk among themselves."

He paused to shoo a young girl out of his tent before she could touch the meat cuts that sat gathering flies on a wooden bench. "Bror Friberg, now, he's the boss man, he'll be the one to tell you. He speaks the Swedish, he's the man that went over to round them all up and bring them back here. He's not a man of words, though, Friberg. He's one of those lusty Vikings himself, of course, but he came out a long time past, before the wars. I shouldn't wonder if—"

Eloise interrupted him. "Where can I find Mr Friberg?"

Sikes's laugh rattled from his mouth along with spittle and bits of his last meal. They were sometimes weeks in the bush at a stretch, the butcher and storekeeper together, and the English girls were a welcome novelty. Mr Sikes seemed to find Eloise particularly entertaining. He reached out as if to pat her on the head but she stepped aside.

"You can't just saddle up your old cart horse and wander off into the bush! You ladies will be lost immediately, if not sooner. There's nothing but the old Māori track going south from here, and you'd go wrong on the first bend. Or drown in the rivers. You can't swim in them heavy dresses you're wearing, you'll be swept down to the gorge and never seen no more by the folk back home who love you. And I'll bet there are one or two of those, eh? Eh, little madam, a sweetheart at home, is it?"

"Did Mr Friberg go with the settlers to Dannevirke?" Eloise asked, not liking the sneering mouth of the man and the way his eyes flicked from her face and down her dress and back up again, as if she were a fold of meat he was contemplating slipping his knife into.

But the butcher wouldn't be interrupted. "You'll have to take your dresses off and swim across in your undergarments, and wouldn't I like to be there to see that! And there are wandering Māori on the track in this bush who have never seen a white woman before. You'll have to watch out for the Māori men. They're so dark you can't see them. Perhaps their eyes, sometimes. Little beady eyes, like berries on a bush. They watch you and watch you and then – poof! They disappear. And then there's another one, and then he's gone. And you are left wondering..." his voice dropped to a whisper, "you are left wondering when ... they will..." He leaned forward and suddenly, to Eloise's alarm, shouted, "EAT YOU!!", grabbing her roughly by the arms and pulling her off the ground. His tongue darted out with a wet slide over her neck.

She shook him off her violently, slapping his hands away, revolted by the feeling of being seized by the butcher and mauled like an animal.

"Mr Sikes! How dare you! Keep your hands off me, sir!" She wiped at her neck with her sleeve.

Martha, witnessing the scene uneasily from the edge of the tent, let out piercingly shrill cries of "oh, oh, oh!" and plucked the rope of the tent so it twanged over and over, rhythmically picking at the scab of her distress.

"Go on, get out of here!" Sikes waved Eloise and Martha away like flies from his meat. "You little madam and your idiot sister. You ask me for help but you won't be friendly? Go on, get out of my tent. You be careful I don't come after you and give you the paddle you deserve."

The Norwegian women had gathered quietly, their faces pale and concerned, but they understood none of it and no one intervened. Eloise gently and with some difficulty extricated Martha from the tent rope and led her back inside to her corner of the barracks, where she sat cross-legged on the floor like a young child and tapped her fingers together, far away in another world.

"I'm going to Dannevirke," she told Lars when he returned in the evening, his body stooped and moving slowly but his face alive with the first sight of her waiting at the edge of the track. "I need to find Mr Friberg."

Lars dropped his working gear in the shed's lean-to and stretched his body up, bending and straightening his knees, pushing his knuckles into the lower part of his back. "He is not there," he said. "He is leaving Dannevirke already for stations. To bring supplies to settlement. He will be here in Te Whiti in few days. You must be waiting here for him. I hope he is bringing good news."

A few days. She wanted to ride out and find him immediately, but they could wait a few days. Lars watched her carefully until she nodded, yes.

"I must see to my sisters. And wash. I am sorry ... it is not nice." He waved his hand to indicate the whole of him and it was only then that she noticed the dark patches of sweat on his shirt and realised she had been inhaling the peaty smell of the forest he brought with him. He was too close; she could breathe him in and hold the scent in her lungs. She found his physical proximity almost overwhelming. He smelled of wood chippings and smoke and something so confusingly deep and complex she involuntarily leaned forwards, but Lars turned abruptly away, almost tripping over his axe as he went back into the open space, as if he could not see where his feet met the ground and had no control over the edges of his own body.

***

A few days passed and Mr Friberg didn't come. Eloise bought a butchered wild pig at a vastly inflated price from the surly Mr Sikes, which Lars and the men spit-roasted, the fat dripping onto potatoes in the embers. All the families took a slice. Eloise and Martha sat on a felled tree and ate with their fingers from a shared wooden bowl.

Martha grinned. "We will never tell Father!" she said, as she wiped her greasy fingers on the grass.

Men from the *Høvding* arrived in the clearing, usually in the evenings, when families gathered around the open fire and the men bought salted meat and basic necessities from the shopkeepers. Few had brought equipment with them from Norway, and they quickly ran up debts for carpentry tools and household goods.

Either Josephine or Lars questioned them all, Eloise and Martha standing anxiously by. Some remembered the sailor who came aboard in Cape Verde, but no one had paid him much attention. It was as if the man had his head down to avoid being seen.

Hemi came and went, back and forwards from the farms on the plains, bringing goods for the store and government rations for the settlers. Always he looked out for Martha, gave her a wave. Mr McCreedy would make the trek back to Napier on Thursday, he told them. Some of the Norwegian women, distressed by the inhospitality of bush life, asked to go with him, abandoning the bleak settlement for the opportunity of work as domestics on farms or in town. Anywhere with a roof over their heads was an acceptable start.

"Martha, you come too, eh?" Hemi brought treats for Martha: apples, a wrap of salted meat. Once a handful of boiled sweets. "You come with us back to Napier, you and Eloise. You need a nice house, not the bush. You'll turn Māori if you stay here."

Martha looked to Eloise. "We need to find our brother," Eloise said.

"Mr Friberg will come on Tuesday," Hemi said. "He can find your brother. You let me take you home."

They had walked a few steps down an open path where the light fell almost to the ground, the start of the road to Dannevirke – the scrub hacked and pulled by the women and children and the trees felled by the men. The debris lay packed between the surrounding trees, making a wide tunnel which ran from the clearing for fifty paces before the trees closed in and the road dwindled to a track. This short road was the result of weeks of labour. The men divided their time between government paid work on the road and work on their own sections, building basic homes and scraping land for a garden.

"Why don't they just burn the bush away?" Eloise asked Hemi.

As they peered up into the glossy branches a fat bush pigeon flew out from the upper leaves and along the path of the new road, its wings beating a low, slow *thwop thwop* through the air. Hemi pointed his hand like a musket and pretended to shoot.

"If you start a burn and then the rain comes? Then you have a land of charcoal trees. You can't use that wood. So, you need another fire. But there is nothing to start a fire with, 'cos you burned it all. My father, Mr McCreedy, he bought a farm out at the coast and had a half-burn. The trees were all on fire but the wind changed and the rain came. Some of the green trees burned and he put in grass but the ash poisoned the soil and the sheep got sick and their wool was no good. Then he couldn't sell the land because of all the big dead trees. No one gives you money for that, for charred trees. You've got to cut the big trees first, then you burn the rest later. Now my father has no farm and has to drive wagons!"

They stopped by a tall, straight tree engulfed front and back by a thick vine that suckered onto the trunk, wrapping its arms around it in a bear hug, smothering the host tree.

"This is rātā, this vine, on a matāi. It starts with a seed high in the branches, then slowly grows down to the ground. Now the rātā wraps around the matāi and they grow together." Where a branch split, Eloise saw the golden yellow flesh of the matāi. The rātā, in contrast, was a dark red plum.

"Look, Martha, they're hugging," said Eloise. Martha was counting the branches.

Hemi, as he walked, had plaited a strand of flax. He twisted it into a circle and gave it to Martha with a smile. "Bush bracelet." Martha took it, but she didn't put it on and had dropped it by the time they got back to the clearing.

Lars was looking for them, rubbing the blisters on his hands, worn and sore in his body. As always, his head went up and he smiled gladly when he saw them coming down the path. Eloise wondered if he had asked Hemi specifically to look after them when he was away working.

"I don't work tomorrow," he told Eloise, holding his hands out as if offering a gift. "I take my sisters to visit our mother. Can I take you with me?"

His expression was so hopeful Eloise thought she might crush him if she said no. "Yes," she said. "Yes, I would like that."

That night, as they sat together by the fire, she asked him why, the first time they met standing by the rail of the *Balmoral* and watched the stars on the equator, he had let her talk and talk and not replied. "I would never have spoken had I known you understood me. A complete stranger. Why did you pretend not to understand? It seemed ... dishonest."

He looked troubled. He started to apologise, to explain, but his words trailed away. Finally, he told her, "You are the saddest face I ever see."

His expressive hands moved again, spreading out, passing something between them. "I have no words. In English, how can I say what it is I feel? Even I speak Norwegian I don't have these words."

He was quiet for a while, staring into the fire that shimmered and sparked. "Not dishonest. But no such words for this. For you."

"No. I understand. I'm sorry. Not dishonest."

As darkness fell, Lars took her hand. It was a simple gesture, but one that changed everything and made their hearts jump and clatter. For a long moment, the time that passes between thunder and lightning, a wave of energy built between them and the world focused there, where his skin touched hers.

Nothing could have prepared her for such intimacy. She felt naked and known. She soaked him in for the time it took to draw a full breath and then gently she removed her hand.

Where his touch had been, there was now a void.

Eloise wondered how dishonest she was being now, with him. His hand lay on the ground between them, an invitation. She clenched her teeth and stared into the fire. When she couldn't bear it any longer, she forced herself up to go and look for Martha.

CHAPTER SIX

Lars's sisters, Britta and Lenne, ran along the path, twirling their arms like windmills, happy to be on the move, happy to view their half-built home for the first time. The track was dry and the bright morning sun cast fluttering showers of light across the path. Lars chased them and danced with them and when Britta grew tired he carried her on his back, her spindly little legs wrapped around his waist and her arms dangling over his shoulders.

"Eloise!" the girls called out to her. "Eloise! It is sunny! It is sunny! It is not raining! It is not windy! It is sunny!" They had spent many lessons learning about the weather on board the *Balmoral.* "Today it is Sunday!"

Lenne took Eloise's hand and swung it high as they marched over the tree roots. She sang snatches of English hymns and what sounded like Norwegian folk songs. She asked Eloise the English words for everything they saw. She was an engaging child with a precocious memory.

They travelled in a straight line on flat ground for a mile or so, but Eloise had no real sense of distance. There were no viewpoints, no variation in the dense bush on either side of the trail. The mountains stacked up westward but could only be seen through the occasional gap in the trees. They passed tracks leading off to the right and left.

"Larsen," said Lars, pointing to a painted sign on a felled tree at the edge of the path, and then further along, "Olsen. Look, Britta – here is Tove's land. Familien hennes bygger her et hus." He explained to Eloise, "The father of her friend builds a house here, near a stream. We are neighbours. Same stream."

They came to a crossing, and turned right onto quite a well-worn path, wider, and with trampled ground as if horses had passed on the track. The mountains were directly ahead, dramatic, cloud-covered peaks above steep blue slopes.

"It is a Māori road," Lars told Eloise, and then translated for his sisters. "It goes to Ngamoko and the mountains. Sometimes, on the road you see them."

"Are they friendly?" asked Eloise, remembering the butcher's warnings. The pathway crossed the stream, where ponga logs had been lashed together to form a rudimentary bridge.

"But yes. They come to visit. We clear trees by the stream, but Māori man say the stream flood high in winter, over bank. He say we must to build house back and leave trees to drink the stream. They help carry stone for our fireplace. We are sorry we have no money for pay and they go away. Then later come back with pigeon for our dinner and to light us fire."

"They were speaking in English?"

"No, in Māori. We are learning!"

"Kererū. Wood pigeon."

"Yes, kererū! And tūī, with white patch here." He waggled his fingers under his chin.

"Mr McCreedy calls it the parson bird. Tūī is nicer."

They could hear the sound of axes as they walked, muffled by the trees, some back behind them and some ahead. Little Britta had been walking the last stretch, but put up her arms to be carried again. Close to home now, both girls were emotional and exhausted after months of travel.

The chopping stopped, replaced by the shouts of Lars's brothers, who had caught sight of the party and came crashing through the trees to greet them. They swooped in and picked up the girls to carry on their shoulders, clapping Lars on the back, unsure of how to welcome Eloise. The brothers were shorter and stockier than Lars, both handsome and clean-shaven, alike as twins. Already they had tree-fellers' arms, sleeves rolled up over pronounced biceps, and strong, square chests.

Eloise followed them down the rough path to their farm and they stepped out into the open.

She started abruptly, shocked. It was a place of hell and destruction.

What had she been thinking? A farm. She had in mind her farm in Cornwall, soft grassy hills with fenced paddocks and stables and a stone house with thick glass windows, a kitchen garden and fruit trees bordering the drive. Of course, that would take time here, but somehow in her mind she hadn't reckoned on the intermediate steps, and the fact that the settlers had no horses or machinery, nor any tools other than the axe. No plants for the garden. No grass and no clear land to sow it.

She gasped audibly and gazed, horrified, at the smashed jungle, for that was all there was. Fifty paces square had been clean felled and the trees lay twisted, dead on the ground, raw stumps bleeding in the sun. On the left was thin scrub; beyond was an open space where the stream cut through in a trench, trampled and muddy where the first trees had been cleared. The desolation horrified her.

Lars's father and mother had their backs bent over, arms wrapped around the branches of a cut sapling, and they heaved it over the debris.

Immediately, Lars and his brothers jumped across and took up the weight and the tree, with their combined strength, slid forwards a length, clearing a space around a wooden structure opposite, facing the sun.

Eloise scanned the site wreckage, but there was no other structure to be seen. This frame of rough-cut poles and mud, this was their home. There were tree ferns tied to the poles for insulation and a tarpaulin lashed to a tree at each end for rain and sun cover. An outdoor fire pit of blackened round river stones was the kitchen. It was worse than the barracks at Te Whiti.

The family had left their home in Norway and emigrated for this, a pocket of smashed trees in this godforsaken, most remote end of the earth.

Lenne and Britta crumpled in against Eloise; Britta took hold of a fold of Eloise's dress and rubbed it against her cheek. Eloise reached her arms around them as they paused on the threshold of the section.

Lars walked towards her and she tried to compose her face but her expression lingered and she could not hide her horror.

"Our farm," he said, sweeping his hands to indicate the crushed forest and broken land. "Our forty acre farm. Our house, here. What, Eloise? You are surprise."

She blushed furiously but there was no smile she could fetch when she imagined his mother, his sisters, living in such conditions. She asked simply, "How will you live?"

He looked disappointed at the question, as if she had let him down. "How we always live. I think maybe you do not understand what it is to be poor."

His parents and brothers had their hands on another trunk and they manoeuvred it over on top of the first. Eloise saw there were stakes in the ground, and that they were building a wall, of sorts.

Finally, they brushed the dirt from their hands onto wretched, torn clothing and the older couple came forwards. Their faces were lined and their hair silver grey, but they stood straight and their eyes were clear. They shook Eloise warmly by the hand and bid her welcome. There were hewn logs by the fireplace, carved stumps chiselled roughly like the beginning of grand chairs, and Eloise was amazed that before they had a chimney or a roof, there was a throne on which to sit a guest.

"Carpenters." Lars pointed to his father and brothers. "Father bring his tools."

Mrs Nilsen made tea, something sharp and smoky that tasted like the bush smelt. Green, heart-shaped leaves in the pot.

Lars spoke to his father and translated for Eloise. "He asks why you here, I tell him you look Matthew. He says Mr Friberg will know."

He spoke to his father again, in the same measured way he spoke English, using his hands to emphasise a point – like this, like so. Mr Nilsen spoke directly to Eloise and Lars translated. "He want me to tell you sorry. Sorry for brother, for Clem. For fever on ship. For to die. And for Billy, who cannot see. And hope to find Matthew. They ask to say prayers to God for you, for family."

Eloise's eyes burned with tears at the love she felt from these good people. She, too, would pray for them. She would pray for health and prosperity and comfort for them in their hard lives ahead.

***

On the way home they stopped at Josephine's family farm, where a small fire had been lit to burn off scrub and make a fertile base for a garden behind their hut. The family was heading back to Te Whiti for the evening meal and Lars asked them to take his sisters on ahead, staying to watch the fire for them as it died down, safe for the night.

The hot afternoon had turned to a calm, clear evening, the stars just visible in the dark blue sky overhead.

Eloise paused, knowing she should leave with Josephine.

"Stay?" Lars asked her. And so she turned back to him and let the others go on without her. Lars raked over the ground with long stick, the warmth from the embers rising up in waves like something material she could run her hands through.

There was a heaviness between them. The next day Mr Friberg would bring news of Matthew's whereabouts. Whether her path led south to Dannevirke or elsewhere, it was unlikely to bring her back to Te Whiti. She wanted to find her brother and return to Napier. To a house with a table and chairs, dinner on a plate and a bed with clean linen. She was weary of the bush, and the hardship and the hopelessness of these people starting new lives from nothing.

They rested for a while on logs by the fire, facing the mountains.

"Tell me your life, Eloise. I think something is wrong. You stay in town, in Napier, not on farm. This is change? I think is difficult for your father to build farm without strong sons to help. This is right?"

He looked at her with his kind eyes and Eloise felt unreserved. She had opened herself to him so fully already, she had no need to pretend; he knew that things in her family were not well. She explained to Lars they'd had a letter telling them there was no farm. Perhaps their uncle had deceived them. He had never bought land, but went to Thames, and her father had followed him – they were old friends. She told him how her father couldn't bear to look at Billy, and claimed aloud to have no sons left. They were abandoned and didn't know what was expected of them.

Her eyes brimmed. Lars moved to sit closer to her. She felt the warmth of him through the light fabric of her sleeve. He was so vital and alive, and she drew on his strength.

He told her, "There is gold in Thames. Perhaps your uncle, he get gold fever?"

"Gold?"

"They find gold in rivers there for long time, now perhaps in ground. Men come from everywhere, over all world. Some find fortune. Most not. I think it is not good place."

She shook her head. "I don't know about that. Father said it was a business venture. I think he has gone to Thames to try to join in the business. Uncle Horatio is not a farmer, certainly not a miner. He was a businessman in New York. But Father wanted land for the boys." The pool of water in her eyes threatened to break. "Only now..."

Lars reached up and touched her cheek. A simple caress, a short stroke of her skin with the lightest touch from the tips of his fingers. Then the palm of his hand rested there, in the curve under her cheekbone, as he drew closer and then hovered, not moving forwards or backwards. The bush around them settled and rustled with the sounds of birds settling, in the trees and in the undergrowth. Twigs fell. Leaves dropped, Eloise alive to every sound. The mountains were dark shapes against the evening sky.

"And there is another thing," she said.

There was a shift, and she felt his balance change, expectantly.

"Another letter. From a man called Cornelius Wainwright." She spoke slowly, dropping her words carefully into the pool of understanding between them. His eyes narrowed almost imperceptibly.

"Cornelius is a cousin of my mother, from home. He has decided to emigrate, too. He will join us in New Zealand."

She was not looking at him now, her hands were in her lap and she was helpless, unhappy. Lars slowly withdrew his hand from her cheek and rested it on his knee.

"And for you, what is Cornelius Wainwright?"

"He has proposed to marry me." Again she spoke with a clear clip on her tongue. She did not want to have to repeat her words. "If we ever are to have a farm, my father needs a son to work alongside him. And he trusts Cornelius." She waited. She couldn't bear to say it. Still, the evening settled downwards and little bits of spent life dropped into the undergrowth. "My father accepted his proposal. I am betrothed." And then, to prevent any misunderstanding, "I will be married to Cornelius Wainwright."

There was no physical change in Lars. He was still, other than his hand, so recently against her cheek, which turned over. He looked at his fingers as if expecting to see gold dust there.

There was an intensity now between them, like pressure in the air before a storm. His back was straight and his shoulders flat, but Eloise felt something slump. The last light of the afternoon, which had crept through the lattice of the trees, had dropped from his face. Any glimmer that came through the forest had gone and he was lit only by the embers' glow.

And she knew then that she had lost him, and the loss was unbearable. So she asked him, "Do you love me, Lars?"

"How can you ask this?" His voice was tight with distress, but she knew he was not surprised at the question. It was a gossamer thread that had hung between them for so long now, the tension pulling and pulling. "You see how I live. I have nothing for you. And you must to marry another."

"But I need to know. Do you love me?"

He raised his eyes to hers and she saw right into him, an unbarred glimpse of his soul. "It will not make you happy, to know this. It is not right I answer."

"I don't care about right. I don't care about being happy. I asked if you love me. Do you love me, Lars?"

He was deep within her eyes now, a hook neither would release. He nodded, biting his lip, and a joy leaped up in her and stampeded off into the night.

"Yes, I love you, Eloise. But now I say this and there is my heart it is gone. But I have to say this. I love you. And now I say this and it is over." He made a circle in the air with his expressive hands as if he held his heart, which he offered to her, letting it go. He stood quickly to leave but she was fast to her feet and stepped with him, taking his hand.

"Then stay here. With me. Just for a moment."

There is a strength in nature that draws things together. A vine around a tree. A bird to a nest. A moth to a flame. He brought his arms around her, her kiss on his lips, their love wrapped together.

***

A heavy summer downpour all night and all the following day left standing water across the southern stretch of Te Whiti and flooded the fireplace. Large tracts of glossy mud spread from where the paths led off into the bush. The mist hung above the treetops, and the mountains, usually such a dominant presence, were beyond dismal sight.

Mr Sikes the sneering butcher had decamped back to Waipukurau, and his friend the storekeeper kept his tent sides rolled down and was out of view.

Eloise was pleased to see the back of Sikes. He watched her unpleasantly, and she had seen him following Martha into the bush once when she went to relieve herself. He had turned away when Eloise shouted at him, and veered off towards the men's space. She knew Martha was frightened of him; she would turn her back to keep him out of her sight. Lately, at the sound of his voice, she had started nodding and talking quietly to herself.

Eloise asked her, "Martha, has that man bothered you?" But the question alarmed Martha, and Eloise let her be. All the women at the camp disliked Sikes.

With the butcher gone there would be no fresh meat other than bush pig, brought to camp by the few immigrants who had guns.

Martha and Eloise stayed dry in the barracks with the remaining children while their fathers and increasingly their mothers worked on clearing and building. They worked their sad plots in thrashing rain, under blistering sun, in whatever circumstances God and the New Zealand Government sent them. It was a bitter end to their dreams of the promised land, an indication of a precarious future.

The children were restless and not inclined to settle to lessons. Some of the girls knitted blankets on whittled needles using wool donated by Hawke's Bay farmers. The ever-inventive Hemi had made a tight ball of vines for the boys and they kicked it around inside the extended hut, making an obstacle course of the mattresses and belongings.

Eloise stood at the door, watching the track in. Waiting.

Finally she heard horses, and Mr Friberg's party arrived. They came with sacks of food and tools and household equipment for the store. The store tent flap opened to the driving rain as the men unpacked and brought the goods in. The horses churned the remaining grass of the enclosure into a mire, steaming and blowing like engines.

Friberg was a handsome man with a thick beard, wide cheekbones, a high forehead and a well-groomed appearance. He nodded acknowledgement to Eloise, who stood wringing her hands in the doorway of the hut, but saw to the horses, instructed the men to unpack and checked paperwork with the storekeeper before coming across to her.

He took off his hat and stepped out of the rain into the muggy atmosphere of the barracks. His gestures were courteous and his blue eyes were kind.

"Miss Sansonnet, I presume." He shook her hand. "I am Bror Friberg. I understand you are waiting some days to see me. I apologise for the delay. We have many settlers to visit here in Norsewood. Where can we talk?"

His voice, although accented, was clear and precise.

Eloise didn't need to look around the barracks to know there was no private space and no quiet corner. Martha pushed aside a mattress by the fireplace and swung away the rack of damp clothes. They stood in a huddle with their backs to the room. Friberg's coat steamed in the heat from the fire.

Eloise explained their quest to find Matthew. Hemi, it seemed, had carried their case forward already. Friberg was aware of the details and came well prepared.

He knew the man Matthew, who had joined the crew of the *Høvding* in Cape Verde on their short stopover, claiming to be an English sailor. He had had little to do with him on the ship, and it was not until they anchored in Napier that the man had approached him.

"What did he look like?" asked Martha. "Did he look like Eloise?"

Friberg shook his head.

"I am afraid not, Miss Sansonnet. He may have a slight resemblance, yes. I see now, how this might add to the confusion. But this man is not your brother."

"Where is he?" asked Eloise. "Is he in Dannevirke? Can we see him?"

"I don't know where he has gone. He went to Dannevirke, yes, but it was never his intention to stay there. He has left the Scandinavians and gone on to find work on one of the farms to the south." He held up his hand to stall their questions. "He is not your brother. He speaks English, yes, but with a strong accent. His identity wasn't uncovered on the *Høvding,* as English among the crew was limited. But when we arrived in New Zealand he slipped in line with the Norwegians and pretended to be one of them. He asked me to take him south, somewhere remote. He wanted to be away from the port, from the militia. I took him because he was a hard worker and a good man, I thought, who deserved a second chance. But I did learn more about him as we travelled. Ladies, I tell you this quietly and in confidence, as it is all the proof I can give you that this is not the man you seek. The man is a German soldier."

"A soldier?"

"A defector. He fled the German army and was stranded in Cape Verde. He saw the *Høvding* and heard she was short-manned and bound for New Zealand, and so he seized his chance. But the boat carried many Swedes. Germany has been at war with Sweden for some time. So he took an English identity and kept his head down. I am sure he will find a way to reinvent himself as an honest settler. I grew to respect him as we travelled, very much.

I am sorry for your loss, but he is not your brother."

It had been a fool's errand. Eloise wondered if she had really believed they would find Matthew tucked away in a remote bush hut with the Scandinavians. Had she merely wanted to believe it, and willed it to be true?

"There is more, though." Friberg weighed his words carefully. "Matthew, of course, is an assumed name. His real name is Heinrich Pfeiffer. But, on the *Høvding,* he wrote his name as Matthew Sansonnet."

"Oh!"

"We have now changed his name to Henry Piper. It occurred to me that the name Sansonnet was too unusual and would be recognised. And so it would seem."

"But he met Matthew at Cape Verde? He took his name? What did he *do* to him?" Eloise had her hands on Friberg's arm now, trying to squeeze the information from him.

"My dear, I don't know the answers to those questions. I am sure he didn't do anything to your brother, if you mean 'do' in the malicious sense.

Heinrich is a peaceful man. He left the army because he didn't want to fight. I knew nothing of your story until Heinrich – Henry – was gone, so I could not ask him. But I can hazard a guess. My guess is that your Matthew jumped ship at Cape Verde to find another passage going in the right direction. Your young Māori friend told me the *Halfwellen* was bound for the Indies. I would go further to guess that, as your brother didn't go south with the *Høvding* or west with the *Halfwellen,* he is trying to find a fast way back to England?"

Eloise nodded carefully.

"And I guess that the two men crossed paths and Heinrich, put on the spot, used Matthew's English name when the Swedish crewman signed him on."

"So Matthew is alive?" asked Eloise, as Martha tapped her fingers together furiously.

Friberg nodded. "It seems very likely. And by now probably on a ship back to England."

Eloise flew to Martha and hugged her tightly, and Martha, stiff as a board, patted her back consolingly. Eloise rocked her from side to side as big gulps of tears and laughter threatened to topple them down onto the straw mattress on the muddy floor.

"And now, if I may make a suggestion, you girls should pack up your belongings and tomorrow morning saddle up that big horse of yours, and young Hemi will take you back to Waipukurau for your journey home."

***

It took them nearly a month to get back to Napier. They were held up in Waipukurau for over a week in Mr Wix's tight hovel while Mr McCreedy ran provisions out to the farms and got caught up on business, and then another week when the wagon lost a wheel in a deep muddy rut and needed a replacement sent from Napier. Mr Wix refused to let them go on to Napier unaccompanied, and now that the urgency of the quest was over, both girls felt drained.

The minister tried to be accommodating, but he was a severe man and especially critical of Martha and her unconventional behaviour. "She hasn't tied her bonnet!" he scolded Eloise, as if she could possibly be angry with Martha for such a trivial thing, after all Martha's bravery and steadfastness on the road.

His tiny house was unfit for three people; they were constantly tripping over each other and got on one another's nerves terribly. The days were clear and sunny, so the girls spent their time outside with Mary or Hemi, who was waiting in town for Mr McCreedy's return and had been put to work by Mary in digging a vegetable patch behind the shack. Martha and Hemi worked side by side, companionably clearing around the neglected orchard of peach and plum trees that served the new ministry. Hemi taught her to milk the cow, an activity for which Eloise thought Martha completely unsuited with her jerky movements and dislike of unpredictable things, but the boy was patient, the animal placid, and Martha was proud beyond measure of her first pail.

Eloise spent nearly all her remaining money in Waipukurau's shops and a local farm. She bought woollen blankets and boots and a dozen live chickens in a raupō basket, which she loaded onto Buttercup and sent with Hemi back to Lars's family in Norsewood. She wanted to send them a cow, but Hemi reminded her there was no grass and it would die. So she added bags of grain for the hens, a sack of clover grass-seed, a trowel, two wooden buckets and a tin tub for washing. In Hemi's pockets she placed two small cloth dolls with smiling embroidered faces and button eyes for Britta and Lenne, donated by a woman of the parish.

Eventually they turned north and began their journey back in the rain, but by Waipawa, first Martha then Eloise got sick, their weeks in wet clothes and harsh conditions taking their toll. They stayed a further week with a Scotch woman, a widow who kept a neat house and cooked well for them, hot broths of stored grain and greens that grew like weeds in her small garden.

Hemi came with them as far as Waipawa, cared for Buttercup and saw them off with Mr McCreedy when they were well enough to travel. He gave them sweet, early strawberries wrapped in a twist of paper. Mr McCreedy sent him back to Waipukurau with a consignment of furniture.

Martha left him without a backwards glance, but Eloise looked back as they rode out of town in the wagon and saw their young companion standing in the road, watching them go.

"He has been a good friend for you, Martha. You are such a strange egg. You've never been bothered with having any friends before and then you spend all your time with a Māori labourer. If I didn't know better, I'd think the poor boy was lovesick. Do look back, Martha! He's standing in the middle of the road. Oh, do wave to him!"

Martha turned and raised her hand briefly, but she didn't smile and was more interested in the road ahead.

Eloise had written to her mother from Waipukurau. She hoped the news that at least they knew Matthew was alive and bound for England would have brought about a change in her, but when they reached Napier they found their mother much as they had left her. Physically stronger on Serenity's good cooking and enforced walks over the hill, but with her heart still gone from her.

"She cries for Clem every day," Serenity told them. "She won't accept that Matthew is safe. Give her time to deal with her grief."

Serenity was patient and careful with her. She had taken the precaution of bringing Doctor Croft back, who prescribed jelly, port and medicinal vapours. He presented a box of Beecham's pills, which Serenity left unused in the cupboard. Penelope remained aloof.

Billy was morose, although he, too, grew stronger and more stable under Serenity's care. His eyesight never improved. There was light and darkness, and blurred colours, but nothing came into focus. He developed a habit of reaching forwards with his hands and grasping at the air. He was at an age where his friends at home would be putting aside childhood and turning to scholarly and sporting ambitions, but school was out of the question for Billy, and his sport consisted of a turn around the town on the arm of the minister's daughter, his hurdles diminished to rocks on the uneven ground. He grew angry and depressed.

From Robert there had been no more than a few brief lines. He had arrived in Thames and found Horatio. They were investigating business opportunities. There was no mention of gold mining, for which Eloise was relieved. There was a small allowance for their upkeep arranged with Mr Duffy at the Bank of New Zealand. They should be frugal until things were settled, he said.

The weeks bumped past. Christmas came and went with little joy, and summer hit Hawke's Bay like a furnace, scorching the grass and turning the hills yellow.

Serenity was away during the day, doing good work with the local Methodists. She continued her visits to groups of immigrants on the hill as they disembarked off the ships, and worked with her Swedish friend Ana, helping to process them into their new lives. Immigrants came to Hawke's Bay from all over the world: America, Australia, England and Scotland, Ireland, Scandinavia, Germany. She recorded professions and skills, and she matched these with opportunities. The colony needed shepherds, wool scourers, fell-mongers, coopers and bailers from the men, and domestics, cooks, even "wives" were required from the pool of women.

The minister's letters came regularly for Serenity in the weekly mail. He complained of the lawlessness of the roughnecks in town, the unwelcoming and isolated farmers, the difficulties of a parish with no congregation. Some local Māori, he said, were better educated than the immigrants; many at least had received the benefit of a missionary school. The labourers and navvies brought in from the West Country were an illiterate and disorderly lot. Serenity, he said, must stay away until things settled.

Occasionally, groups of souls came looking for Serenity at the house in the evenings and she invited them into their parlour. She was gaining a reputation as a lay preacher, and went to the Bible Christian Society meetings, where her simple faith and compassionate sermons touched many.

Eloise went out with her on occasion and took Billy and Martha. The local women offered sympathy and patted her condescendingly, but Eloise couldn't help noticing that conversations stopped when she entered the room, and the women clucked like hens. The poor wee girl with the absent father, mad mother, blind brother and sister with the twitching affliction. It was only a matter of time before they learned of the brothers dead and missing. Eloise hated their pity. She began to avoid gatherings and took her exercise with Buttercup, riding into the hills or along the waterfront, her mind far away. Always south, always in the bush, always with Lars.

Martha picked up a stomach bug and was bedridden for a while, and Eloise was again confined to the cottage to nurse her sister. Martha's stomach grew tight and swollen and she couldn't hold down her food. The sickness came and went, but Eloise decided against contacting Doctor Croft. They knew themselves by now how to administer cold cloths and herb teas.

Eloise wrote to her father, care of the hotel in Thames, the only address she had for him. She knew not to question him directly, so she asked for instruction. Should she pay a man to bring barrels of drinking water from the well, as their neighbours did? There had been no rainfall for several weeks, they had no tank water left for washing and the garden was dry. Ought she arrange a tutor for Billy? They had nothing to spare on their allowance and both Billy and Martha needed new boots. There was good news that Buttercup, despite the sea voyage and poor stabling, appeared to be in foal. What should she do?

He sent no reply.

Eloise turned to Serenity in frustration. "What am I supposed to do? We are abandoned here and I can't help Mother when we are so unsettled! Why has he left us here, Serenity?"

Serenity could only offer the distraction of those more in need, the truly destitute.

"Come with me this afternoon," she pleaded. "Martha is better today, she can look to your mother and Billy. I am preaching over the hill in Ahuriri. There is a charity house on the causeway where women live, women who have been truly abandoned. They need help, Eloise. They need to find a way up from where they have fallen."

But Eloise didn't have Serenity's strength or goodness, and she recoiled. All she knew of prostitutes was that they were among those who had fallen from God's grace and were therefore not worth saving. She listened to Serenity's arguments about the redemption Christ offered everyone. Prostitutes, too. But for Eloise, visiting the house was a step too far. Serenity went to the causeway alone. She came back late in the afternoons filled with grief for the women and shaking with anger at the men who, so casually, caused such suffering. She wrote letters and attended meetings.

Women's suffering continued unabated.

In the new year there was a letter from Cornelius. He had booked his passage and would leave in April to join the family. He eagerly anticipated working with father and sons on their

Hawke's Bay farm. Robert, it appeared, on accepting his suit for Eloise, had neglected to mention their changed circumstances, their lack of a farm, the tragedies that had befallen all three of his sons.

If she thought of him at all, Eloise was anxious to have Cornelius among them. They were a house of women and poor, blind Billy with no security. Her father rarely sent letters and answered none of her pressing questions. They were unable to move forward without a man to make things happen and Eloise felt frustratingly powerless. The stores would not offer credit, workmen would not take employment from a woman and Mr Duffy was unable to negotiate their allowance without Robert's approval. Someone had to make Robert come back and take charge of the family.

Her betrothal to Cornelius was something that Eloise left fluttering in the air, unconsidered, a long way off. Her childhood friend had faded with distance, and now she could barely picture his face. Marriage could wait. Without Matthew and Clem she felt so helpless. Cornelius was a poor substitute for her brothers, but he had been her friend all her life and she needed him.

She soon forgot all about Cornelius. Long before he arrived, their lives took an unexpected turn.

***

February was hot and dry. The days dawned with the sun rising over the shining pale blue sea and setting with the bleached hills aflame in a rich, intense light. The remaining trees around their small settlement were cut down for development and there was nothing to hold the heat at bay. The soft, silver skies of Cornwall felt more than a world away, as if they had never existed at all.

Napier shook and bustled with activity. Men strode purposefully around the town and public works were carried out energetically. Construction on the roads and railway was rampant, and constant noise rattled the streets. Ships trailed their wakes in and around the harbour: tall-masted immigrant ships, trading vessels, Māori canoes, coastal steamers and local lighters connected the hinterland, through the bustling port, to the world.

One morning Martha had a sip of tea at breakfast, left the room and was sick in the garden, bile streaming from her lips over the carrots.

It was Serenity who guessed the truth. Once it had been suggested, the signs were indisputable.

Martha was with child.

Of course she was. Her belly was growing round and she had long given up lacing. Her morning sickness, her dislike of certain foods.

Eloise looked at her sister in horror.

How could this be? How could this possibly be?

She told her mother immediately, passing the responsibility away.

Penelope smiled for the first time in months and her eyes lit up in wonder. She seemed to step back into her old shoes, the mother from the past who was warm and kind and alive.

"Is she now? Is she to have a baby? Oh, my little Martha. Oh, that's wonderful! She'll have to eat to keep up her strength." Her voice had returned to her as though from a long time asleep.

Aghast, Eloise took her hand. "Mother! We're talking about Martha. Your daughter Martha. She's barely seventeen. She's a child. And she won't tell us how she came to be this way."

But Penelope was ecstatic. She got up in the mornings of her own accord now, to take care of Martha. She laid her clothes out for her and sang snatches of folk songs and old lullabies to her, comforting tunes and rhymes. Martha abdicated all responsibility for looking after herself, and Penelope asked no more of her.

It was a strange and shocking time. They didn't know what to do, how to cope, what it meant. Martha's sickness stopped and she began to bloom. She went back into the garden and started clearing the ferny bank to make a herb patch from their boxes of seeds, energetically pulling the deep roots and standing triumphantly over her small incinerator at the end of the day. She appeared so healthy they put off calling the doctor, frightened of the damage he might do and the scandal it would cause.

Serenity explained to Eloise and Billy, clearly and honestly, how a woman became with child. Martha was not married; a man must have forced himself upon her.

But Martha either didn't remember or wasn't telling. She wasn't upset. Her tics and restlessness had calmed. After a day scrabbling in the garden she sat reading in the evening, smiling to herself with her hand on her belly.

There had been immigrants and travellers in the hotel with them that first dreadful week after arrival, when they been shattered, each wrapped in a web of grief and loss. Billy was horrified that something had happened to Martha and no one had protected her. "Did someone frighten you at that hotel?" Billy asked her in his new deep voice as they sat in the sun on the small verandah. When he pressed her more specifically about men in the hotel corridors or the wash room she didn't understand him. Bewildered at the tone of the conversation, she walked away.

Eloise thought back through Martha's on-and-off days, the panics and the nerves. Many days since leaving Cornwall Martha had been distressed. So much was new and frightening, and when confronted she put her head down, tapped, sometimes argued quietly with her demons. There was no point trying to touch her or talk to her. They all knew it was best to make a wall around her to protect her from the outside world and give her space. She had been happy in Te Whiti, where no one confronted her or expected her to speak, and she had done her chores in silence with the Norwegian women singing and chatting around her.

With disgust, Eloise thought of the butcher in Te Whiti, Mr Sikes. He had set Martha off when he caught Eloise in his strong, fat arms and licked her. He had called Martha an idiot. Eloise remembered being uncomfortable about the way he had watched Martha, who had been afraid of him. But all the women in the camp were instinctively wary of him and kept him at a distance. Was he capable of such a thing? Eloise couldn't believe that something so distressing could have happened to Martha without anyone realising. They had been surrounded by women and children.

Sick with the idea, she asked Martha if Mr Sikes had ever touched her. To her horror, Martha said bluntly, "I hate him."

"I hate him, too," said Eloise gently. "Can you tell me what happened? Did he hurt you?"

"He followed me. I hit him." Martha's eyes widened and she smiled triumphantly.

"Martha!"

"That's all, Eloise. Nothing else happened. He went away."

"Martha, you are going to have a baby. A man put the baby inside you. You need to tell me if it was Mr Sikes. No one will be angry."

"Mr Sikes didn't put a baby inside me. That's disgusting."

She gave a light laugh but her shoulders twitched and she started tapping, lightly, on the arms of the chair. Eloise brought her a blanket that she had started knitting for Serenity's immigrants, and her hands fell to the steady click of the needles. Eloise let her be.

One afternoon, Penelope had her hand on Martha's belly and felt a movement. She held Martha's hand and together they waited for the movement again. The two women, mother and daughter, exchanged a look, Penelope smiling and Martha unreadable. Eloise noticed a change in her sister, her pale face looking no longer defenceless but powerful, glowing. She had put on weight and her arms were stronger, her cheeks filled out.

Eloise recognised something in Martha's face. It was joy.

As she regarded her sister, a memory unfolded to Eloise. She remembered Martha in Waipukurau working in the orchard with Hemi. She had worn the same face then, of joy, a light source trapped behind her eyes giving her a self-contained radiance.

Perhaps Martha hadn't been attacked by anyone. Perhaps she had lain down willingly behind a bush with a native. Good God.

Her mother was asking Eloise a question, and raised her voice to ask again. "Eloise! I said, can you get the cradle from the attic? We'll need the cradle for Martha's baby."

"From the attic, Mother?"

"Get Matthew to help you..." Her voice trailed off and she scattered glances helplessly around the foreign room, the attic-less house.

Serenity came home with a midwife, a practical motherly woman who, she told them, had twelve children of her own and twenty-one grandchildren. The doctor, they all agreed, would not need to be involved.

There was no discussion on the morality of the situation, no question that they would do anything other than allow Martha to keep the baby. Their shame, here in the colony where they had no roots and saw no future, was a soft thing.

Eloise did not write to tell her father, and if Serenity gave the news in her letters to the minister, she did not share his reply.

Slowly, the summer passed. There was no great show of autumn; the days got shorter, but most of the trees remained stubbornly green. Then the drought broke in March with torrential downpours that turned the cliff behind them into a waterfall, and a rockfall collapsed onto a nearby house. It was miserable to exercise the horse and there wasn't enough left in the allowance to keep her stabled, so Eloise took her to graze for the winter at a farm in Clive owned by Mr Rowe, one of Mr Duffy's Acclimatisation Society friends. She came back from the village in a Māori canoe, feeling adventurous and wild.

Out of Napier, away from the confines of the house and the care of her mother and Billy and Martha, Eloise allowed her mind to wander free of her charges and remember. She remembered being on the road, the carts going south with the Norwegian women, the terrible, terrible disappointment they faced when they confronted the reality of farms that were nothing but bush with years of impossible debt. How poor they were. And yet how good the people. Her mind kept going back to the day with Lars when she visited his mother and found her bent double pulling a tree trunk, and how she straightened her back and put the tin pot on the open fire and made Eloise welcome with bush tea. This strong woman went about doing the daily things, looking after her children, making the meals, knowing that poverty was relative and it was good enough to be alive.

And Lars. She simply closed her eyes to picture him – in the bush with muddy breeches and sleeves rolled, remembering his manly smell of earth and physical toil. She tried to imagine him in her world, washed and groomed and dressed in an evening suit in an elegant drawing room, but it was a fantasy that felt flimsy and unreal. She wanted to remember him as he was, up a tree with his axe or hauling timber through the bush or strapping poles together for a fence or a bridge; working, always working. She was sure, in his mind, he was holding her close. She felt warm.

CHAPTER SEVEN

Serenity Wix was a popular lay preacher in the new church on Emerson Street and she had a dedicated party of regular followers. She still held her simple services for the immigrants at the barracks on the hill, and one Sunday afternoon, when a cluster of ships was in port, she performed an evangelical service in the open air of Clive Square and drew a crowd of over a hundred worshippers.

She believed in goodness, and goodness followed her. She held events for the benefit of widows, orphans and the destitute, and the Napier ladies fought to offer her membership of the Education Movement, the Women's Charitable Aid Society, the Ladies' Benevolent Society. Serenity tried to introduce Eloise to these groups, but Eloise resisted, uncomfortable with the society of the parochial town, not knowing where she fitted in. A displaced Sansonnet with a broken family was out of sorts with the natural order of things and the good women of Napier seemed to find it difficult to fit her into the context of their lives. She flinched at their pointed questions.

Billy often went out with Serenity. She took him to the church hall on Thursdays and the Benevolent Society rooms on Fridays. It was easier for the women to ignore a blind boy to his face, and he felt no obligation to talk to women he couldn't see. Serenity placed him at the piano while she gathered her books and arranged chairs and Billy felt his way over the keyboard, trying to pick up by ear the pieces he used to sight read so fluently, relearning chords in the dark. It came slowly. Often he grew frustrated and would pound the keys in anger, not knowing or caring who was in the room.

One afternoon, a Miss Belle came to sit by him, and added some chords to a melody he was picking out. She was a piano teacher from Dorset, a spinster of around thirty, newly arrived with her grandfather and looking for a project.

"I'm not a project," growled Billy, but Serenity told him not to be ungrateful and encouraged Miss Belle to persevere. Slowly Miss Belle helped

Billy find another way of playing, a new way to learn. She began to teach him to read the music with his ears.

He refused to play for the congregation and Serenity didn't press him, but found him a chair where he could sit with Miss Belle. She was pleased to hear him join in the singing, his voice lifting sweetly and then dropping uncontrolled into its new, deeper register.

Occasionally, and deliberately, Serenity invited her ladies to the Sansonnet home. If the ladies had opinions on her living arrangements with the abandoned mother and the now obviously pregnant girl, nothing was said to Serenity. She encouraged Martha to walk out of the house every day for exercise, and told Eloise to hold her head high on the street.

"Look them in the eye," she told her.

"I will, Serenity. I am a Sansonnet!"

But Serenity held up her finger and told her, "Not because of who you are, but because you are good and kind and have done nothing of which to be ashamed."

One day, Eloise went to see Mr Duffy at the bank. He invited her proudly into his new office, sat her down and offered tea. He had been promoted and they had moved into a larger house on Tennyson Street and were thriving, he said. It was when Eloise asked after his Cornish starlings that Mr Duffy's smug face slid from his cheekbones. The starlings had disappeared! All of them, flown off inland somewhere, and the crops were still riddled with the dratted caterpillars.

"What did they think would happen?" he asked her. "They held a ceremony in the botanical gardens. The chairman of the Acclimatisation Society himself opened the cages and the birds simply flew away. Of course you can't pluck birds from the hedgerows of England and transport them halfway around the world and expect them to fly up and roost in your chosen trees," he said in exasperation. "They're birds! Unpredictable by nature. Uncontainable. I always said the chance of any good coming from that experiment was very unlikely."

Eloise remembered the starlings' fast choreography over the Cornish meadow, that last summer. She hoped none of her starlings were ever transported and released here, muddled and lost and unable to find their way home.

Mr Duffy asked after her health, her mother and Billy, and then he reddened with embarrassment. The tea arrived in time for him to avoid having to ask after Martha.

Eloise held his eye.

They had bills to pay, she told him. She didn't mention the baby, but they needed blankets and a crib, money for the midwife. They needed boots. Their allowance simply wasn't enough.

Mr Duffy grew increasingly uncomfortable. Of course he could do nothing without Mr Sansonnet's approval.

"Mr Duffy. Has my father been in communication? Can you give me any news?" He was a good man, thought Eloise, and had been kind to them since landing. He struggled to hide his discomfort. "You do realise that my mother is unable to conduct any of the family affairs. She is ... indisposed. I am here on her behalf. You can trust me with any news you may have, Mr Duffy."

He shook his head miserably.

"My father does not answer our letters," Eloise told him, with exasperation. "We don't know what to do, or how long this will go on."

"I am sorry to say that Mr Sansonnet does not entrust me with information of his affairs. I cannot tell you the nature of his business. I can't authorise anything. I must have his approval for any transactions."

"Perhaps we can sell something? Can we sell our books, or Mother's furniture?"

"As Mr Sansonnet's banker I cannot interfere. Perhaps Mr Wix could persuade him to return?"

Eloise snorted. She did not need to say that the preacher held no sway over her father. She needed practical help. "Can you recommend a buyer for our possessions?"

Mr Duffy wrote down the name of an auctioneer and ushered her out. He walked out into the street with her and, once off the premises, shook her hand

and leaned in to say, quietly and clearly, "Most of the money your father came with has gone. He removed a large amount a few months back. Invested in what, I don't know. I do hope your father is taking good advice."

***

By April the intense summer heat had dispersed. There was warmth in the daytime but as the sun moved north the cold shadow of the cliff fell across their roof and by early evening the house was chilly.

Eloise had a letter from Mr Rowe to tell her Buttercup had foaled, and she decided to take a trip to Clive to see her.

"Leave Billy at home with me," suggested Penelope, but Eloise disagreed, saying he needed to get out in the world. From the river's edge a dishevelled waterman rowed them across the lagoon and up the Tūtaekurī River. Once aboard the dinghy, Billy turned his face to the new sounds and smells.

"You know, Eloise, if we overturned now, I wouldn't know in which direction to swim to save myself. There could be a bank right by my elbow and I might swim the other way."

"Well, you'd hear Martha splashing. I'd rely on you to save her."

"Do you remember when I tried to make you learn to swim? We were at the river with Clem and you asked me when on earth you would ever need to swim."

"I remember, Billy."

"Here's when."

"Give him a push, Martha."

"Really?"

"No! No. I meant frighten him. Don't actually push him in, silly."

"Tell me what you see," said Billy, so Eloise described the flat listless sheen of the water and the shingle and mud banks. There were wading birds pushing their long bills into the mud and gulls pattering about, circling the one gull who had something in his beak. They could hear the surf close on their left but not see through the swampy vegetation that grew over the spit of land that separated them from the ocean. Ahead was the bare bony ridge of hills that looked like a giant lying down.

"It's the sleeping giant," said Eloise. "Has Serenity told you the legend? He is the ancestor of the natives here. He was from a tribe over on the coast and loved a local girl. Her father made him eat through the hill to prove his love, which seems rather harsh. So he bit a big chunk out of the hillside but choked and lay down to die. Do you see where he bit?" She pointed ahead at the gap between the hills.

"No."

Eloise squeezed her eyes shut at her stupidity. She saw Billy slumped, with his eyes closed. "I'm sorry, Billy, that was for Martha. Do you want to know more about the local tribes?"

"No."

His good spirits returned at the farm, where Buttercup gave a soft whinny of recognition and Billy could rub his hands over her familiar bulk and learn the shape of her foal by feel. He rested his head on her flank. "We'll keep the foal, won't we, Eloise?"

But there was still no more money from their father, and the foal went to Mr Rowe for Buttercup's keep.

They sold the sideboard to buy a large carpet to keep out the draughts and enough firewood to last them the winter, and they tightened their belts, all except Martha, who continued to grow a big tight belly under her smock. They gathered around the kitchen range in the evenings, and Serenity's small church stipend was spent entirely on food.

Winter came with a blow and a downpour, but fell short on its threat. In Cornwall the first winds were the prelude to cold and snow, but the Hawke's Bay winter temperature stayed well above freezing, bright days returned and the winter greens in the garden continued to grow with surprising vigour. Eloise and Billy walked out every day, through the town to the church, where Eloise left Billy at the piano and did her errands. Occasionally, when she returned to collect her brother she found that Mrs Duffy had dropped into the church and left some scones with Billy, and once, a small jar of golden honey. There was something tragic about the handsome young man bent over the piano with his eyelids drooped. His playing was less disciplined than it had been at home, where he had flown lightly over the sheet music. Now he drew his music from a deeper well. He gained a small group of admirers, fluttering young women drawn to vulnerability.

Martha went into labour in the middle of June. Eloise counted nine months from their stay in Waipukurau. One morning Eloise awoke to find her sister moaning, her bed soaked and Martha with her arms wrapped around herself, rocking in pain.

The baby was slow to come. Billy was sent away to the church, out of the way, and when Miss Belle brought him home in the evening the baby had still not arrived and Martha was screaming and crying.

Eloise pleaded to send for Doctor Croft but the midwife told her in a calm voice that there was nothing the doctor knew about a girl giving birth that she and Penelope between them didn't know and hadn't felt. The midwife sensed that the key to Martha's comfort lay with her mother, so she took Penelope's hand and guided it over Martha's belly and below the great mound, talking reassuringly to both mother and daughter. "It's coming," she said. "It takes a while, the first one."

Serenity made them eat a late supper and then she, Billy and Eloise sat helplessly in the kitchen by the fire, the noise of Martha's cries and moans overhead.

Eloise woke with a start in the middle of the night. She was asleep on a blanket on the floor, stretched out with her back to the fire.

There was no sound.

For a few moments, she wondered why she was there, on the floor, why was there no moonlight from the window, why the room was so small. She was in her childhood bedroom and she'd been playing with her toys on the rug and fallen asleep.

She turned to look for Martha in her little bed, but she was in a strange place and there were sleeping bodies around her lit by the glowing embers of the fire.

She surfaced slowly.

Not a sound came from the upstairs room.

The screaming had stopped and everything was dead quiet in the dark house.

A raw, nasty taste of bile hit the back of her throat as she realised what the silence meant.

Not Martha. Oh, dear God, not Martha, too.

She tumbled over and crawled across the room, pulling herself to her feet on the doorframe and staggered up the stairs. In the little back bedroom she shared with Martha she saw bodies on the bed.

"Martha! Oh no, dear God, my darling!"

"Quietly now!" said a gentle voice. "Shh, girly." And the midwife, in the chair by the door, removed the shield from the lamp and turned up the wick.

"Come and see."

Eloise took the lamp across to the bed and looked down at the bodies in its warm yellow glow.

Three sets of eyes stared back, blinking at her. Martha and Penelope with almost the same face, one blonde haired and one grey, eyes blue and ringed with exhaustion in pale angular faces. And between them, lying on Martha's fragile white collar, a big brown baby with shockingly black eyes, round as buttons, under a scrap of black hair.

***

They finally asked Doctor Croft to visit, to record and register the birth. He recorded the baby as nameless and fatherless.

The doctor advised he knew of no formal adoption agency in Hawke's Bay, but suggested there were women without children on farms where an illegitimate baby could be placed. Perhaps the church...

Penelope turned her back on him. It was Serenity who explained that Martha had decided, with the full support of her mother, to keep the baby in the family.

As Serenity showed him the door, the doctor argued with her. "It's not the right thing to do. Goes against all convention and moral decency. She will never be accepted. The Sansonnet family don't want a bastard child. For all their unusual circumstances, the family are good stock. The church will never accept it."

Eloise saw Serenity's back stiffen and her head went up. At that moment Eloise loved her absolutely. "God will accept her," Serenity said in a voice so utterly convincing that the doctor held up his hands, nodded and bowed to her as he backed away.

For the next few weeks they were cocooned in the little house, all of the family taking turns with the baby they named Winnie, a big, healthy girl, while Martha, poor wrecked Martha, regained her strength.

It was Eloise who told Billy the baby was native, as the boy sat with his niece tucked comfortably into the crook of his arm.

"How do you know?" he asked. He had never seen a Māori. "Is she very brown?"

"She's the colour of those eggs your hen used to lay – remember ours were white and your hen lay those huge brown ones. She's the colour of your eggs. The colour of a cinnamon stick. Nothing like the bluey white of ordinary babies. And she has a very round face."

She was a bonny thing, her nose a beautifully curved line. There was a sculpted indentation beneath her nostrils, and her lips lifted like a wave's crest. Her ears, velvety soft, curled like shells.

"She is altogether delicious."

"I wish I could see her," said Billy. He nuzzled his nose into her ear and blew gently, and the baby tucked her chin down into her fat little neck.

"She likes that," Eloise told him.

Hesitantly, Eloise had broken the story of Hemi to her mother and Serenity but now, after Winnie was born and there was no doubt, she asked Martha to tell them.

"It's Hemi's baby, isn't it, Martha? Will you tell us?"

Martha was more peaceful than she had ever been. She was heavy and lethargic. The big sack of her belly hung loose under her extended dress and she sat in the chair with the baby at her breast, focusing intently on the scrunched little face as she suckled.

There was no twitching. Martha's fingers, holding the baby so carefully, were still.

"Did you love Hemi?" Eloise prompted, and her sister nodded, yes.

"He is a half-caste native labourer. He drives a cart," Eloise told Serenity and Billy, as they left Penelope, Martha and Winnie in the house and strode up the steep hill in the fresh air. "How could she do this? Has she no shame?"

Billy, his hand on her arm as she strode up the barren road, was struggling to keep up. The hillside was being cleared for housing, other than the stretch kept for the scrappy civic gardens that sloped down to the town. They stepped up past the cemetery to the barracks, along a road with pegs marking sections where piles of timber were laid ready for housing. Eloise wondered if the timber came from the Seventy Mile Bush, if any of the axe marks had been made by Lars.

"You can't judge Martha like other people," said Billy.

"Oh, don't you tell me what Martha understands," replied Eloise sharply. "She's helpless and stupid when it suits her, but she's no fool. She knows what is right and what is a sin."

"That's for God to judge," said Serenity. "Not you."

"I should never have left them alone together!" cried Eloise. "How was I to know she needed a chaperone? He was her chaperone! How could he take advantage of her like that?"

"How well did you know this man, this Hemi?"

"Oh he's just a boy, hardly a man, yet. I thought he was harmless. She'd never had a friend before, and he made her laugh. How often have you seen Martha laughing? He drove the wagons, carried the settlers' goods, always made sure Martha had what she needed. Brought her little gifts." Eloise kicked a stone up the road. "How well can you know a Māori?" she asked bitterly.

She remembered seeing Hemi off when she sent him back into the bush, high on Buttercup, laden with chickens and blankets and the fundamentals she prayed would keep Lars and his family alive in their desolate isolation. Hemi had gone willingly, as if on an adventure, proud to be of service. He had been gracious and kind. She hadn't paid him. She didn't remember thanking him. She hadn't treated him well.

When they reached the barracks there were children waiting to greet them, stamping their feet on the cold gravel and blowing clouds of steam into the sharp air. Their little faces were pinched and they still had a look of the sea about them. They walked with small steps in contained circles. They were English and Scottish, newly arrived and waiting for settlement.

They flocked around Serenity and held her hands, pulling her with them. The Swedish woman, Ana, opened the door and brought them in out of the cold.

"It arrived," she said, and pointed to an alcove where, pushed up against the shelves stacked with boxes and oddments, was the Sansonnets' piano. "Your piano, Billy," she said, and led him around the refectory tables, pulled up a chair and played a note for him.

"My piano?"

"We couldn't afford the storage, Billy," said Eloise, "and it won't fit in the house. Mother wouldn't sell it."

She watched her brother's face carefully for a reaction. "It's just a loan," she added.

"So the immigrants have music," said Billy, and he nodded slowly. Then he shrugged. "Oh, well. It's no use to anyone in a box."

Billy pushed up his sleeves, spread his fingers dramatically on the keys and dropped heavily into a chord. B Flat minor. The start of a funeral march.

They left him fingering the keys, muttering about the pitch of the lower notes, the children knotting at his elbows as he ran up and down some scales and entertained them with sudden, loud chords.

Ana gathered the women together and Serenity took reports on their journey, the families' health, concerns for their children.

Eloise drifted. In an adjacent room one of the older girls was looking after a newborn and two older babies. Eloise took the crying infant from her to give the young girl's arms a break. The change of position gave the baby pause, but soon her cries started again and

Eloise walked back and forwards, rocked side to side. She sung and whispered.

The carer, a young Cornish girl called Sarah, changed the cloths on the other babies and the stench filled the small room.

"You get used to it," she told Eloise, and Eloise knew she would. She opened the window to clear the air and the girl wrapped and cleaned and took the soiled cloths to the laundry.

Sarah came back wiping her hands on a fresh towel. She put a clean pile of cloths on the table by the cot and gave the baby a kiss on the head.

"That one's always been a bit teasy. She's just been fed, she's not cold. She's always unsettled. Born on the ship, she were." Sarah's voice came straight from home, the rich vowels and slurs so reminiscent of the farmyard that Eloise felt a grab of nostalgia, a deep hole of loss opening in front of her, and she had to turn away so the girl didn't see the tears in her eyes as she stumbled. She stood by the window and looked over the yard as the baby in her arms gulped huge lugs of air and sighed and quietened. Eloise rested her lips on the tender head, breathing in the new baby smell which, like Winnie's, had the slightly sweet flavour of pancakes or warm fire stones.

They joined the others for the service, the sleeping baby back in her mother's arms and Sarah now enfolding an older child on her lap, who was sucking on a strand of dull brown hair, her face locked into the ship-shocked expression Eloise recognised from her own travels.

Serenity spoke simply of God's love. She preached of the need to be honest and true to his spirit and to seek honesty and truth in fellow men. She spoke of compassion and the forgiveness of sins. She suggested they not mumble the phrases handed to them but examine their faith and take responsibility for their own salvation, to make the words a part of their lives. "Read your bible," she said. "Even if you are far from civilisation and your nearest church is two days away, God is with you. You will find Him in your bible. Understand the words. There is nothing worth living for that does not promote the cause of God. Hold God in what you do, every day."

The children sat quietly now, all faces turned to the slight figure of the preacher as she stood on the bare boards of the crowded barracks in her one dowdy brown dress with the patched hem, and spoke with such passion.

"This one thing I do, forgetting those things which are behind and reaching forth unto those things which are before, and I press towards the high calling of God, in Jesus Christ."

Billy, at the piano, began to play. It was the introduction to a hymn they knew well. It wasn't one that Eloise would have chosen for these good people, but it tied them tightly to home where still, every Sunday, the verses would rise from churches all across Cornwall. Serenity, Eloise and Billy began to sing and some of the Cornish women joined with them, sweet voices filling the crowded and messy room with peace.

Where shall my wondering soul begin?
How shall I all to Heaven aspire?

*A slave redeemed from death and
sin,
A brand plucked from eternal fire,
How shall I equal triumphs raise,
Or sing my great Deliverer's
praise?*

*Outcasts of men, to you I call,
Harlots, and publicans, and thieves!
He spreads His arms to embrace
you all;
Sinners alone His grace receives;
No need of Him the righteous
have;
He came the lost to seek and save.*

*For you the purple current flowed
In pardons from His wounded side,
Languished for you the eternal
God,
For you the Prince of glory died:
Believe, and all your sins forgiven;
Only believe, and yours is Heaven!*

They stopped on the way home to
buy bread for lunch from Fred Sutton's
store at the foot of the hill. Their debt
in his little shop grew, but the man was
in awe of Serenity and he wouldn't ask

for settlement from the Sansonnets while she accompanied them. They walked back down the lane into a sharp winter breeze that blew off the sea.

Through the window, they saw an official-looking man standing in the drawing room. He was tall and well postured, his chest out and hat in his hand, his formal dress stiff and new.

Penelope came through from the kitchen with the tea-tray. The man made no attempt to help her.

Eloise opened the door from the street and the others followed her into the drawing room.

"Eloise?"

The tall stranger looked a bit like cousin Cornelius, from Cornwall. He, too, appeared unsure of her. The pair regarded each other for a suspended pause.

"It's Cornelius Wainwright," said Penelope quietly, as she put the tea-tray on the small table. "I've made him some tea."

***

Penelope was dressed in her oldest, plainest shift, with her gardening apron wrapped around an untied waist and a napkin over her shoulder. They were all clothed pitifully. Their visitor had dressed to call at a gentleman's house and found the family in work clothes. It hadn't taken long for the colonies to rub the velvet off.

They could hear Winnie fretting in her basket and Penelope picked her up, still swaddled, and held her over her shoulder to rock her.

Eloise registered the transformation. The rather sweet, soft-cheeked and bumbling Cornelius Wainwright had somehow turned into a fairly stern-looking gentleman, in a smart double-breasted frock coat and striped grey pantaloons. His whiskers had grown and were well trimmed and his face had matured. He looked unexpectedly dignified. His eyes, though, were the old Cornelius's eyes, hesitant, tentative. *Does she like me?* they always asked. *Am I doing the right thing?*

Eloise was at a loss.

"Won't you sit down?" she asked him.

He was staring past her now at Billy on the doorstep, who was smiling into the room but not advancing. Cornelius obviously sensed something was wrong but couldn't pick it, and he appeared to wait for the old Eloise to throw back her head and laugh and tell him that he had it all wrong: that this shabby, reduced family was a play they were rehearsing, or an elaborate joke.

But the old Eloise had nothing to say.

Billy came forwards and held out his hand and Cornelius was forced to meet him halfway and look him in the eyes. Eloise saw the jump as Cornelius recognised that the boy was blind.

"Hello Billy, it's good to see you," he said, and then grimaced at his faux pas.

"Well, lucky you," replied Billy nastily, and then a moment later he crumpled slightly and tried to undo the damage. "Sorry. Blinded by the fever, you weren't to know. It seems there may be things you weren't told, and I'm sorry for you, Cornelius. This isn't what you expected. But look, here it is.

Here we are. May I present our companion? This is Serenity Wix."

And so they perched uncomfortably in the room and had tea and ate little biscuits that Mrs Duffy had made and Eloise told Cornelius how the Sansonnet family had fallen apart.

"Will you walk with me?" Cornelius asked Eloise as he rose to leave. Billy came as chaperone and the three walked down Carlisle Street into the town.

Cornelius puffed and rubbed his whiskers and started to speak several times, tripped over his words and reverted to tutting and shaking his head.

"I think you should say what is on your mind, cousin," said Billy. "We have obviously upset you."

"Oh, I am upset!" spluttered Cornelius. "This is not what I expected on my arrival. Not what I expected at all."

"Why would it be?" responded Billy angrily. "We didn't get what we expected either. Everything went wrong the moment we left Cornwall. We should never have left home." Eloise pressed his hand on her arm firmly.

They stopped at the corner and waited as a large wagon was pulled slowly past by two horses, piled high with imports from the docks. The driver swore as one of the horses stumbled in a hole in the road and Eloise recognised the driver, Mr McCreedy. She kept her head down.

"I will write to Cousin Robert immediately," said Cornelius. "He wasn't straight with me, you know. I have been misled. Deliberately misled. I know not why. Where is the promised farm? Why are you left with no man in the house, what is this business of your father's that keeps him away? Why was Martha asleep in the daytime, is she sick?"

He pulled at his coat cuffs as if he hoped to straighten the whole mess out with a bit of good tailoring.

"And why on earth was Penelope looking after a baby?"

They left Cornelius at the Masonic Hotel on the waterfront. At last, as he said goodbye, he broke the restraint that had sat over them like a thick afternoon fog and Eloise heard the voice of their old friend. "Eloise, Billy, I am so sorry for your loss and my sympathy for you is heartfelt. I will mourn Clem like a brother. Your distress is my burden, too, you know."

Eloise and Billy walked on, awkward together now, both silently contemplating their transformation through the eyes of Cornelius Wainwright and realising how far, indeed, they had fallen in their expectations of colonial life.

They visited Mr Duffy at the bank. He looked up with pleasure when they arrived and came out of his office to greet them. For once, he had good news.

"You will need to bring your mother down to see me, my dear," the kindly man told Eloise. "I will need her signature. There has been a significant change in your situation. Your household account is well stocked and your father has agreed to a substantial increase in your allowance."

It was good news, of course it was, but it left Eloise uneasy. Mr Duffy could tell them nothing about the type of business in which Robert was engaged, nor did he have any news of Robert himself. There were no instructions on what they were to do with Cornelius now he had arrived, or what was expected of him. Robert's address was still a hotel in Thames. Good news, surely, would be something in which they all could share, and yet there was nothing forthcoming other than the money to keep them.

CHAPTER EIGHT

Cornelius visited once more before leaving Napier for employment on a sheep station out on the coast. He had received a letter from Robert advising him to establish himself locally while Robert and Horatio grew capital to invest in land. Cornelius was aggrieved not to be included in the partnership but at least he had a profession to turn to in the meantime.

"He's counting sheep again," said Billy to Eloise, when he thought Cornelius was out of earshot.

"Oh, hush."

For Eloise, Cornelius being a few hours ride away was ideal. She wasn't ready, yet, to explain Winnie, and was relieved when he left without asking for further clarification. He wrote weekly with news: he was well employed, they were opening up land for pasture and increasing stock. He wrote at length about the requirements for a good breeding program, most of which, when reading his long letters aloud to the family, Eloise skipped over. His employers, the Collinses, were what he termed "New Zealand gentry", and he suggested the Sansonnets could look to them for inspiration. In less than twenty years Mr Collins had turned wasteland into a thriving farm of 20,000 acres; he had established schools for the natives and his name was on the foundation stone of the Methodist church at Waipukurau. Cornelius was ambitious for his new life as if he, too, were only a few short years away from the pinnacle of his aspirations.

Cornelius did not mention the other thing, the promise that had brought him from home. Eloise was relieved and let it lie.

Serenity saw him once. She had begun travelling with her father on the Wesleyan Methodist circuit and their district included Clive, where the Collinses came to hear her, bringing Cornelius with them.

"He didn't recognise me at first," she told Eloise. "He wasn't listening to my sermon, but was attentive to his friends, the Collinses. They are good people. I imagine Cornelius went along to be polite."

"But you spoke to Cornelius?"

"Indeed. He surfaced when he found Mrs Collins befriending me and I reminded him of our acquaintance. He told me he enjoyed my lesson very much, which was kind but decidedly untrue. I can recognise an inattentive face in a congregation."

"I'm sure you don't see many."

She smiled. "He may have felt a bit at sea. It's a mixed service compared to what he would be used to in Cornwall. Perhaps he prefers a more formal division between the Methodists. There are some who don't approve of the general blending of the Wesleyans here."

"Did he offer an opinion?"

"He did ask if it were only the Methodists who have become so liberal. So I told him that we are all very liberal in New Zealand, at which he looked a bit shocked, as if I was talking about things other than the church. I explained to Mrs Collins that the old Methodist Church building in Napier went to the Catholics at the Mission, and we were actually standing in a Presbyterian Hall, so we were all a bit looser with our boundaries. She agreed that things that would have been shocking in the Old Country have a different resonance here."

"That is so true," said Eloise, "but I'm not sure Cornelius is particularly flexible in his thinking." Serenity nodded at her to go on. "I haven't told him about Martha's baby yet. Oh, Serenity, I haven't told Father, either. We are all going along pretending it's quite natural that Martha should have a little Māori baby at her breast. If Cornelius found your sermon shocking, what will he think of our situation here?"

"And yet," said Serenity, "you and your mother and Billy, and Martha of course, all seem to be coping with the shock of Winnie very well."

"Winnie is a baby. She is an innocent, of course we all love her! What Martha did was utterly wrong, but God will judge her and I believe He is a forgiving God. Who am I to say what is shocking? Perhaps, when one takes a step off that narrow path of righteousness oneself, the shock seems less relevant than when one is standing by and judging others."

Serenity raised her eyebrows and waited for elaboration, but Eloise shook her head.

The following month, when the Collinses came into Napier for supplies and to hear Serenity preach again, Cornelius accompanied them. He wrote to Penelope. He would not call on them at home, but expected to see them at the Sunday Service. Particularly Eloise. He mentioned that he looked forward to introducing her to his employers.

Penelope put the letter down. "Do you have some sort of arrangement with Cornelius Wainwright, Eloise?"

"Father has betrothed us."

Penelope was aghast. "Why wasn't I informed?" It was the first time in the year since Clem had died that Eloise had heard real surprise in her voice.

"Mother, you were told. Cornelius sent a proposal by letter soon after we arrived, when Father was so lost without Matthew and Clem. Father asked him to come."

"And you are betrothed to him?"

Was she? Eloise wasn't sure. "Cornelius has not spoken of it directly to me. But Father has not told me otherwise so I assume it is still true, yes."

The fire went out of Penelope. She tapped the letter against her palm a few times as if in an attempt to focus, but Eloise saw she had dipped below the horizon again. Her mother disappeared away through the window, across the small town and out to sea.

Sunday Service was in the little hall on Napier Hill, where Serenity spoke again to a packed congregation. She stood on a raised stage at the front, a plain, slim girl, modestly dressed, with a moon-shaped face and dark eyebrows. She had something out of the ordinary about her, but it was impossible to pinpoint exactly what that was. Many people had come some distance to see the girl transform.

When Serenity spoke, the congregation hushed. She spoke without papers, without referring to her bible, in a voice that was low but easily carried across the hall. There was a rhythm to her words that held her listeners in a trance. She spoke of love for children, love for family. She quoted from James 1:17: *every good gift and every perfect gift cometh down from above, from the Father of lights.* She was, Eloise realised, telling Cornelius about Winnie.

Billy slipped from the pew and Miss Belle led him to the piano as they stood to sing. His hooded eyes looked forwards at nothing, but he heard the room and played to the congregation. Eloise saw there was nothing of the child left in him. Their little baby Billy was never coming back. For all his recent rudeness and anger, he was at peace there on stage in front of all the judgemental townsfolk, behind his piano.

He played well.

When Eloise came from the hall into the sunlight Cornelius was there waiting for her. She took his outstretched hands. He had made an effort with his dress and was well scrubbed. There was something in him that reminded her a little of Matthew, a family resemblance on her mother's side, the long neck and proud bearing.

He introduced her to the Collinses with a proprietary air. She shook hands politely, chatted about the service, agreed with Mrs Collins that Serenity

Wix was as earnest and eloquent as any man. She introduced Billy. Their mother and Martha, she said, were indisposed.

On impulse, Eloise invited Cornelius home to lunch, and he accepted immediately. The Collinses left to do their shopping.

"Billy is staying behind for a piano lesson with Miss Belle, and Serenity has church business, so why don't we walk on ahead? I know Mother will be delighted to see you."

So Eloise and Cornelius walked through the town, unchaperoned. He questioned whether this was a New Zealand custom, that unmarried women could be quite so free.

"Mother doesn't like to go out of the house," she told him. "And Martha is occupied with the baby."

"Baby? What baby?" he asked, as if he had no memory of the baby he had seen in the house.

Eloise took a deep breath. It was her chance, then, to test him. To see how much of Serenity's words of love and grace had entered his spirit. In that breath, Cornelius failed some unknowable test. Eloise found she couldn't trust him.

"Oh, she is one of Martha's projects," she said, without breaking her stride. "Serenity has us all doing charity work, you know. Billy plays the piano at services, I work with the new immigrants and Martha helps with orphans. Serenity is persuasive. She'll have you raising money for church funds by the end of the afternoon, mark my words. Now, tell me about you. Where have you been?"

They fell easily into their old roles, Cornelius as the informal family guest and Eloise teasing him in a sisterly fashion. There was something that could have been formed then, perhaps, but she brushed it aside. Smoke in old embers that she couldn't bring herself to blow into a flame.

***

"Mother's more settled now the garden is in order and we have bought new furniture. We have a girl, Daisy, to help with the fires and the cleaning, and her mother cooks."

Eloise wasn't sure why she was chattering on to Cornelius, shining a retrospective golden light over their lives. Cornelius had always come to them in Cornwall as the poor relation. His father was Penelope's cousin, who died before Cornelius was born. His mother had remarried a Wainwright, who had children of his own. There had always been the air of the unwanted about the boy. But Robert had liked to have him around; Eloise had noticed that her father was more relaxed when their cousin had visited. Robert had looked more kindly on Matthew during his visits, perhaps appreciating his son better when compared to his cousin.

Eloise found her relationship with Cornelius now stuck as it had been in their youth, with his role that of a somewhat disconnected member of the family to whom they had an obligation. Part of that obligation had always been that the Sansonnets were happy and welcoming.

Serenity and Miss Belle joined them for lunch, a beef pie with potatoes, which Daisy and her mother handed out from the kitchen.

Miss Belle apologised that Billy hadn't had a lesson that day after the sermon, as her grandfather had arrived to tune the piano. "He was impressed with Billy's playing," said Miss Belle. "Which is quite something, from Grandfather. He tuned the piano in the Albert Hall for thirty years and listened to all the masters play. Usually ... well. He can be terribly dismissive of young players. He's never taken a shine to any of my pupils before." Miss Belle smiled at Penelope. "But he enjoyed listening to Billy. 'He hears the music,' he told me."

Billy was pleased by the praise. "He let me help him with the tuning, Cornelius. I've not been inside a piano before. I tried to feel the strings vibrating with my fingertips, but they all felt the same to me. So Mr Belle let me strike the keys while he tuned. Have you ever seen inside a piano?"

Eloise felt a quick stab of jealousy at the way Billy turned to his cousin so easily for praise. It was a habit he'd had with Clem and Matthew. Do you like it, Clem? Have you seen this, Matthew? Searching for reassurance from his older brothers. Now he sought approval from Cornelius.

"I don't think I have, Billy, no."

"And then I played chords for him to check he had it right. It made such a difference. I thought the dreadful sound was me, but it turns out it was the piano all along."

"I enjoyed hearing you play at the service today," said Cornelius. "I was very proud of you. The Collinses specifically asked to be introduced to you."

Eloise knew Clem and Matthew would not have been so kind. The habitual scowl had gone from Billy's face and Penelope smiled. Eloise mouthed, "Thank you," across the table at Cornelius.

Later, Penelope laid out the sheet music they had brought from Cornwall to sort through with Miss Belle, humming snatches to Billy and Serenity. Cornelius joined Eloise standing by the front window. Outside, they saw Martha walking with Winnie across the small patch of grass with her uneven rocking gait, the baby so well wrapped against the winter cold she might have been a bundle of shawls.

"Martha has bloomed," said Cornelius. He sounded surprised. Cornelius rarely noticed Martha, as if she was a problem for Penelope or Eloise to mind, no business of his. He rarely instigated a conversation with her; he didn't expect anything in return. "She was such a thin, nondescript little girl beside you in Cornwall and I know your mother worried about her health and, well, her capabilities. She's undergone an extraordinary transformation. She looks bigger, and purposeful. Is it the New Zealand air?"

"Perhaps it is," was all Eloise would say. Martha did look well. Relaxed. Happy. Winnie brought out the best in her.

Cornelius was preparing to leave when Martha came back in, Winnie still swaddled and asleep on her shoulder. He patted the bundle gently, the way one would pat a puppy. Martha stepped back.

"I imagine there are many abandoned children in this country of immigrants," Cornelius said to Martha.

"But tell me, why have you taken in this baby? Is there no orphanage that will take it?"

Martha turned her shoulder and put her head down into the bundle. "She's mine." She said it quietly, but Cornelius heard.

Eloise felt the spirit of every woman in the room gather up and circle around the baby protectively. Cornelius frowned. Confusion came and went from his face – a brief encounter with the unthinkable that was quickly dismissed.

"Your devotion does you credit, Martha, that you take your commission so seriously. Jesus said, 'Suffer the little children to come unto me'. Your charity is humbling. Well done."

He rode away on his smart horse back to his business and the women shuffled their feet and looked at each other with guilty relief.

***

Cornelius was forgotten as soon as he was out of sight and it was a month before he wrote to say he would visit again. It was on a Saturday, but Penelope didn't order anything special for dinner and the household continued their usual routine without altering plans for him. Cornelius could fit in, as he always had.

Eloise and Billy had planned a morning walk, and went up the pass between the hills and along the winding track to the top of Bluff Hill, right at the eastern edge of the headland. Billy stood with his face to the sun and stretched out his arms.

"What's in front of you?" Eloise asked him.

He tilted his head.

"It smells tangy. The wind is on my face, it's coming upwards. I can hear seagulls below us. What is in front?"

"Nothing!" cried Eloise. "You are at the top of a cliff and there is only wind between you and miles and miles of ocean. Can you feel it?"

"I can almost see it! There is a light blue colour and it's very bright. I can smell the salt on the wind."

"Careful, you'll fall!" And she grabbed him and tumbled him backwards, laughing. He was a long way back from the edge. They lay on the grassy bank, Billy with his face up to absorb the sun's heat, Eloise propped up on an elbow, looking over the treetops to the sea. The sky arched above the hill with a density of blue Eloise had never seen at home.

"I wish Clem were here," Billy said. "Or Matthew. Remember how Matthew used to put me on his back and we'd go charging around the farm? They could carry me pick-a-back here and I wouldn't have to stumble around everywhere."

"Well don't expect me to carry you around, you big lump."

They fell silent. There was a fantail in the tree, calling a frilly trill, sweet peeps punctuated with high-pitched squawks. Such a different voice to their Cornish birds. It fluttered and flew close to investigate the reclining humans, its tail spread as it balanced on a shrub by Billy's foot. Eloise loved the inquisitive little birds, the cheeky way they dived about the undergrowth, watching people, opening their feathered fans for balance and perching with their heads to the side, as if they couldn't quite believe their eyes. Billy would never see a fantail. Eloise had tried to describe the birds to him before, but he had cut her down. "What's the point?" he had asked.

He was less caustic now. Time with Miss Belle and her grandfather, away from the household, had opened up a new focus for him. Perhaps, even, a bit of hope.

"What do you think will happen now?" Billy asked her.

"What do you mean?"

"We're here, but nothing happens. We're waiting, every day the same as the last. Father has been away well over a year and gives us no indication of the shape our lives are to take. What are we waiting for? Where is this promised farm?"

Eloise pulled a blade of grass and spun it in her fingers.

"Oh, right," said Billy, when she didn't reply. "Yes, we all know what you are waiting for. You're waiting for Cornelius to marry you, and then you can go off with him. Perhaps his wonderful Mr Collins will sell you some land on his vast estate. But what about us? What do we do for the rest of our lives? Do you think Father is ever going to come back?"

"Oh, Billy, I don't know!"

"Does he ever write? Does Mother hear from him?"

"As far as I know the last letter was months ago, telling us there was plenty of money in the bank to buy whatever we needed. I read it aloud, you remember. I don't think there has been anything since. Mr Duffy never has news, he seems to know nothing about the business."

"What is Father's business, is he with Uncle Horatio?"

Eloise slapped her hand down on the grass in frustration. "I don't know! I sometimes wonder if Uncle Horatio even exists! Whatever they are doing is obviously going well. Mr Duffy seems happy with the money coming in. I don't want to go back to that pitiful allowance again."

"Nor me."

Eloise observed her brother closely, staring in a way that wasn't possible with a sighted person. He was so open, lying on his back with his face to the sun, always vulnerable. She closed her eyes and felt immediately helpless. She sat up to look around them. Billy needed her protection; her job was to look out for dangers. For the rest of his life, Billy would require a guardian. Of course that was why he wanted to know what the future held. His trust in her needed to be absolute.

Billy was exploring the same topic.

"Are you honestly going to marry Cornelius and go off with him? I can't imagine you married."

"I suppose so."

"What sort of answer is that? 'I suppose so.' Don't you like him?"

"Oh, of course I like him. I've always liked him, well enough. I suppose I can't imagine being married, either."

Actually, she had been thinking about Cornelius that morning. She was hoping to get him alone for a while after lunch, perhaps for a walk along the front, so she could understand a bit more about what her own future held. Things were so different from when they parted in Cornwall. Cornelius had been Matthew's friend, really, always struggling to keep up with him, though

Matthew was the younger by a year. Cornelius had always been a bit of a bumbler around her, never quite finding the right words at the right time. They had both changed. She rather liked the change in him. He was more dashing now than he had ever been at home; he had grown his whiskers and lost his plumpness and had a healthy look to him. His engagement in the new country so quickly had surprised her, and it was a positive sign that he had found work with a respectable family. Perhaps his lower status didn't mean so much here and he, too, could rise fast. You couldn't tell, with the settlers. Who knew what his employer Mr Collins had been, back in England?

And he did remind her of home. Achingly, poignantly, he brought the past with him. He was silver skies and dewy fields and the smell of wet soil in the morning garden. He was starlings in the trees and daffodils lining the river bank in spring. She couldn't imagine marrying someone who wasn't from home. How could she possibly understand them, or they her?

Of course, Cornelius was still a bit pompous. As children they had teased him for his startled rabbit look, the mask he wore when surprised and unsure how to respond properly. He would put his ears up and blink until he knew whether to be affronted or to laugh. But that collective, "as children", no longer applied. Matthew and Clem were gone, Martha never read anyone's expressions anyway and Billy couldn't see them anymore. Cornelius was her link to a past that had collapsed.

Eloise and Billy walked back down the winding track and arrived home at noon. Cornelius's tall horse was blinking drowsily in the shade at the side of the house, looking like he had been standing there a while.

***

When Eloise pushed open the front door the sun speared a finger across the threshold in a blaze and lit up an item positioned in the hallway.

"Oh!"

Sitting on smooth feet, golden wood glowing in the sun like a throne, was a small rocking chair. She saw immediately that it was made from two different woods fused together, a plum red and golden yellow, burnished to a high sheen. In a flash she was back in the forest of Norsewood and the hugging trees in the bush, rātā and matāi, growing entwined. Could a craftsman have scooped a chair out of their blended trunks? How extraordinary! The seat and armrests were polished smooth, but all around the chair were carvings of leaves and ferns in the many different shapes of the New Zealand bush, long spiky flax and small serrated beech leaves.

With a cry of delight she grabbed Billy's hand and led him to the chair to explore the woodwork with his fingertips while she explained the colours and the shapes in a breathless voice.

The chair's seat was irresistible. Eloise turned and scooped her dress aside, put her hand on the armrest and sank down, letting it embrace her. She rocked back so only the tips of her shoes remained on the floor. The balance was perfect. The chair could have been built for her.

"A young Norwegian man came earlier and left that chair for you."

Penelope had heard them come in and now stood in the doorway.

The breath caught in Eloise's throat and she slowly lowered the chair to level.

"What?" she whispered.

She was aware of Cornelius joining Penelope in the doorway but she only had eyes for her mother.

"He said it was a gift from his family. That they all had helped make it. To thank you for the chickens."

Lars had been here. Lars. He was always there with her, the blood in her veins, under her skin, his head dropping towards hers and his grey eyes climbing into her soul. Never more than a heartbeat away but always hidden, never on the surface. And now to Eloise it was as though suddenly the smooth wood of the armrests under her hands were Lars's arms and he was holding her, loving her, as he had by the fire in the forest.

She held the feeling so tightly she couldn't breathe.

Penelope's voice was tender, her voice from the days when she still had love and hope and carried God with her. "I don't know what you did for that man or his family, Eloise, but his esteem for you was clear. I remember these people from the voyage. It seems your kindness saved his family. You have made me proud."

"Where is he?"

Cornelius stepped into her line of sight.

"Good morning, Eloise."

"Hello, Cornelius. Mother, where is he, where did he go?"

Cornelius coughed, but Eloise's attention was all on her mother. Cornelius said, "The immigrant dropped off the chair and left over an hour ago. I told him to leave it there for you. He's gone, Eloise. He didn't stay."

And when Eloise remained poised on a forwards rock of the chair, Cornelius added, "I didn't invite him in."

She was gone out the door, running swiftly down the path. She looked up and down the road, as if she expected Lars to be right there, on the roadside. She was tying her bonnet as she ran off in the direction of the wagon yard. Behind her she heard Cornelius's shout and the slam of the gate as he followed her.

"Eloise, stop! Eloise!"

Cornelius's steps closed behind her on the road but she didn't wait for him. She wished he hadn't followed her. She had no explanation to give him. If Lars was still here, she would find him and put her head against his chest and have him wrap his arms around her. He had come to her. It didn't seem possible. The bush was so far away, in another life, and yet he had come and left her a gift of such richness that she knew, she *knew,* that to make it he had to have been thinking about her every single day. What did that mean?

Cornelius caught up with her in Clive Square Green as she turned away from the railway yards, heading for the depot where the wagons came in. He wheeled around and stood in front of her, forcing her to stop.

"What are you doing?" He sounded more amused than angry.

And as she made to go past him, he followed with, "The boy said he came by carriage. Would you like me to escort you to the carriage stop? Look, you can see it from here, there is no one there. Your carpenter friend is not there."

Eloise felt deranged. Lars had gone. He had been so close, but he had met Cornelius and left without waiting for her.

The only people visible were two heavy-set men on horseback on the road out of town and some Māori women by the river with their canoes. Eloise's head snapped around back into the town streets. There was no one else in sight. It was Saturday midday and people were indoors, out of the sun, having dinner. There was no blond head, no tall young man with a jaunty stride coming along the road towards her.

He had been to the house, and she had missed him. She deflated, and Cornelius led her to a seat at the edge of the green. "Rest And Be Thankful" was painted in gold on the green bench.

Eloise tucked a strand of hair in under her bonnet and saw, across the square, a labourer digging new flowerbeds. He had boxes of colour and he was slowly and methodically filling the border. The flowers belonged in an English garden under a gentle sky. His primroses and petunias wouldn't thrive in the harsh southern sun.

There was a rocking chair at home that Lars had made for her and he had come all this way to deliver it. She had something of him in her life that she could touch, every day. A declaration made of wood.

The feeling of Lars welled up inside her like a spring. She knew it had never gone away, that he had bitten her with his love and she would carry him in her veins.

Cornelius remained standing. "I think perhaps you owe me an explanation." His voice had a sharper edge now.

"Do I?" She didn't want Cornelius there. Lars had nothing to do with Cornelius, they belonged in different worlds.

"Who is this man, this Lars Nilsen?"

She remembered Lars had asked the same question as they had watched the fire go down and the stars come out in the bush. "And for you, what is Cornelius Wainwright?"

It seemed so long ago.

"Do I have a *rival?*" Cornelius sounded dubious. He tapped his fingers against the side of his leg. He was waiting for a reply but she wished she didn't have to say it. She wanted to keep Cornelius and Lars in separate bubbles.

But Eloise was not a girl who liked secrets. She didn't want her relationship with Cornelius to be based on a lie. She simply couldn't say that Lars meant nothing to her, and yet she could no more explain the feelings he roused in her than she could rip her heart from her breast and hold it up for him to see. So she turned it around on him.

"Are you courting me, Cornelius? Because if you are not, you have no right to ask me such a question."

His fingers stopped tapping and his startled rabbit face appeared. He had no answer ready for her. She felt a bit sorry for him. Cornelius was, in truth, one of her oldest friends and she wished he were more like her brothers. She wished he would sit down next to her, take her hand and ask, as Clem would have done, "What's it all about, El? Talk to me."

But that sort of understanding wasn't in Cornelius's repertoire.

He shifted his feet, confronted and uncomfortable. He took off his hat and for a minute Eloise was terrified he was going to drop on one knee, here, in the square, but to her relief he rubbed his head and put his hat back on.

"I have written to your father on the matter. I cannot discuss any arrangements without his approval. Unfortunately, I have yet to receive a reply."

It seemed not to occur to him to ask whether she wanted to be courted. Eloise knew that Cornelius and her father would come to an agreement and she would be assigned the role of Cornelius's wife, or not. She didn't need to have an opinion because her opinion was of no consequence.

Serenity was the only person she had ever met who believed that women, one day, would have the right to choose whom they married. Serenity believed that women would have jobs, make decisions, vote. To Eloise it sounded a marvellous idea and she had listened avidly, but thought such a transformation of society was unlikely.

"We will discuss this later," Cornelius said. "You are distressed. Allow me to take you home now."

He took her arm and led her up the dusty road back to the house.

Through the afternoon the chair sat in the hallway and Eloise felt its pull. As soon as dinner was over and Cornelius had gone she had Billy and Daisy stagger with it up the stairs and place it in her little room, by the window. She didn't come down for tea. She knelt beside the chair with her eyes closed and let her fingers explore every inch of the carved wood, every joint and fold of the frame, the weight and the heft of it and the feel of the wood under her body as she curled in its lap and lay enfolded long into the night.

The next week, Cornelius didn't visit, but sent a note to tell them he had taken a month's leave and was on a ship to Thames. He was going to talk to Robert face to face.

On the day Cornelius's ship left from Napier, a letter arrived from Robert himself.

CHAPTER NINE

"I have been making enquiries of the shipping companies, hoping for news of Matthew," read Eloise. *"It grieves me to impart this information by letter, it is not the sort of thing one ever wants to write or receive."*

They were sitting in the shade on the back porch: Eloise, Penelope, Martha and Billy. Daisy laid the table for tea, and disappeared inside where it was cooler. It was Eloise who held her father's letter and she lowered it to her side as if her arms had no strength for the flimsy bit of paper. She needed help with this. She felt a sudden need for Serenity, but her friend was in town, on one of her missions.

"The Halfwellen *was lost in the North Atlantic two months after we left her. She never made the West Indies and with no further information, is recorded as going down with all hands. I wrote for confirmation and the reply has taken nearly a year. I did not want*

to worry you with the news until I was sure. Now I feel I cannot go on without unburdening myself to you. There has been nothing more. There was no record of a Matthew Sansonnet on board. There are no ship's logs, nor mention of him in any letter or report. He is assumed lost."

Matthew had been lost to them since that dreadful morning on the *Balmoral* when they woke without him on board. But he wasn't lost in the way her father meant. Eloise's mind was too cold to work.

Billy asked the question. "That would have been after Cape Verde, though? Where he went ashore and met the German soldier? Of course, it is dreadful for all those men, the explorers and the sailors, but Matthew was no longer on board. Was he, Eloise?"

Had he gone back on board the *Halfwellen?* Or taken a ship back to England? How would they know?

Eloise was shocked that it had taken her father a year to tell them that Matthew was drowned, whether the news was confirmed or not. Shocked, too, that her mother had not written to tell her husband what they knew from Mr Friberg, that Matthew had been seen ashore, alive.

Her family was entirely broken, with all the things they didn't tell one another.

She read further. Her father was coming home for a visit.

"A visit?" asked Penelope.

"That's what he says, Mother."

"What does he mean by that? How does a man visit his own household? Is my brother coming with him?"

"There is no mention of Uncle Horatio. Father writes: '*I will take the steamer to Auckland in a few days, and then find a ship to Napier.*' He doesn't say how long he intends to stay."

"Poor old Cornelius," said Billy. "He'll probably see Father disappearing over the horizon from the bow of his ship as he is sailing in."

"Perhaps we should stop calling him Poor Old Cornelius," said Penelope. "He seems to be doing well enough for himself." And then, more quietly, "I wonder what Robert wants?"

Martha, as usual, was oblivious to the conversation around her. She had Winnie on her knee, the baby unswaddled in the heat with her plump little brown hands on Martha's pale arms. The two of them stared intently at each other.

Eloise wondered how they were to reconcile her father to the fact that, in his absence, his youngest daughter had given birth to a native baby. Her mother reached out to stroke Winnie's lush dark brown curls, and Eloise guessed she was thinking the same thing. She would be pleased to have her father home again, but wondered about the impact it would have on her mother.

***

Eloise saw him from her upstairs window where she sat in Lars's chair, rocking and looking out at the sky. She had a book on her lap but she wasn't reading; her hands fell down the sides of the armrest and traced the carvings in the posts. She felt herself surrounded by undergrowth: spiky grasses, fat fleshy leaves, ferns curled with mathematical precision. Lars.

Across the road she recognised her father. He put his bag down and peered over at the house, his head pushed forwards as if he was short-sighted.

Eloise ran downstairs.

Penelope was in the kitchen, sorting peas for one of Martha's experiments. More than anything Eloise had done to bring Penelope back to life, it was Martha's eccentric gardening procedures that got Penelope outside and engaged in living again, and for that, Eloise was grateful.

She had four groups of pea pods laid out on the table, each group grown from a different compost, and was measuring them and checking for blemishes and making notes. They appeared all the same. Eloise paused for a moment and watched her mother from the doorway as she measured and wrote neatly in the almanac Eloise had given her at Christmas.

She wondered what her father would see when he came through the door. Not this – the peacefulness of a gentlewoman bent over a domestic task, her hands working smoothly and her face relaxed. He would see an old woman. Penelope had aged dramatically in the two years since Cornwall, when she had worked her own garden, harvesting seeds and packing crops to replant in a foreign farm. None of the crop seedlings had survived transportation, but of the seeds planted, Martha had managed to bring many to life in the small town garden, eking another generation from the ancient strains.

Eloise went over and put her arm around her mother. There had been no discussion about Robert's arrival, no plans made or food prepared. His clothing had come from storage but still lay in boxes in their bedroom, never unpacked or aired.

"He is here, Mother," Eloise said.

In Cornwall, her mother's habit had been to put down her task, remove her work apron and go to greet Robert at the door. Often her civil enquiry on his day was rebuffed and he would walk right past her, but Penelope had still made the effort, every day, to greet him.

Now her hands paused, with a pencil in one and a pea pod in another, and she looked anxiously towards the door. Her hair, loosely tied in a messy bun at her nape, was almost entirely grey and her face had lost tone, her skin soft and threaded with fine lines across her neck. She wore her gardening dress, with a heavy kitchen apron made of leftover cloth.

"I will go," said Eloise. "Take your apron off, Mother." And she shut the kitchen door behind her. She called for Daisy, who was changing the linen upstairs, and sent her to help her mother prepare herself, and she waited in the hallway for the knock on the door.

Eventually, she went to the drawing room and pulled back the curtain.

The road was empty. She turned her head and saw her father, bag on his shoulder, walking slowly away towards the town.

She wrapped a shawl around her shoulders and slipped out of the house.

***

Eloise reached her father in Clive Square, where a few weeks before she had been confronted by Cornelius asking whether he had a rival. Now she was the one doing the chasing.

"Father, stop! Father!"

Today, however, was a weekday and the town was busy. Her voice didn't carry. There was a building going up on the far side of the square next to the stonemason's shop and a steam-machine thumped posts into the ground. Workmen, unloading a wagon, were shouting instructions to the driver to go forwards, whoa! Hold steady!, and the solitary gardener had finished planting his gaudy floral row and was now arguing with a heavy-footed tree-planting gang who had walked over his beds.

Eloise came up swiftly behind her father, reached out and touched his arm. A whiff of pungent carbolic soap covered a deeper, rancid smell. He flinched and pulled away as he swung around, and Eloise started back, shocked at what she saw on his face.

The expression hung there for a second, a despair like poison on the cracks in his lips and a weight on his cheeks, dragging his face down. There was a bitterness in his eyes, the anger and irritation of a misplaced man who didn't expect to find the road home.

Then recognition.

"Eloise?"

The frown lifted and the face changed as fast as a cloud releasing the sun. The savage stranger was gone, and her father came back. He looked tired and travel worn, but the joy on his face was real and his eyes widened with pleasure as he regarded her.

"Oh, my girl, look at you!"

He dropped his bag, the anger replaced with wonder and he held out his hands to clasp hers, his cheeks lifting all the tension away in a beaming smile.

"Eloise, it does my heart good to see you. You look so well!"

The noise in the square didn't quieten, but they stood with hands clasped and the pleasure between them grew.

"Where have you been, Father, why have you stayed away for so long?" Her voice was sincere, not accusatory. She had missed him. Her life, all their lives, had been in limbo without his direction. For as long as she could remember her father had dictated and controlled what they did, how they lived. Now he was back, she could hand over the responsibility that had burdened her for the last year, the decisions that she and Billy and Martha had muddled out between them. She had been distressed that he wouldn't ever arrive. To have him here, finally, she felt nothing but relief.

"Oh, Eloise, why indeed! When I should have been here with you. But listen, my girl. Look at me. I am just off the boat and it was a rough passage, you know I don't travel well by sea. I am in no fit state to meet your mother today. Give me a day to regain my legs and clean up and I will be with you tomorrow. How is that?"

"Tomorrow, Father? For lunch?"

"Yes, my beauty. I will come at noon, and I will not look such a vagabond."

She let him go and went home to make arrangements.

The next day, when he arrived, the household was ready for him.

Penelope had put on a clean day dress and greeted him at the door, and Robert stooped, rather nervously, to kiss her cheek. A look passed between them, things unknown, things unsaid. Eloise, watching, couldn't fathom it from either side and she stepped back, embarrassed. Her delight at having her father home would not necessarily be reflected in her mother, she knew, but she was upset to see the guarded look back on her mother's face, the dropped eyes, the sad downturn of her mouth. She had opened up since the birth of Winnie. It had been a slow process, drips of water coaxing a dry plant back to life.

Without discussion, baby Winnie was explained in the same way she had been for Cornelius – Martha was helping with the orphans. Robert showed little interest in either the baby or Martha and between them they kept Winnie quiet and out of sight in her room upstairs. We will tell him, Eloise told the family. Just not straight away. He will grow to love her and then we will tell him.

They settled into family life.

Robert went out during the day, for meetings he said, and he spent time at a gentlemen's club on the front.

He turned aside any questions on their future, and would only say that he and Horatio had some business that was progressing well. There was no mention of the family joining him in Thames.

"It's a mining town," he said. "It has a rough and temporary nature."

"Do you have a gold mine, Father?" asked Billy, and Robert gave him a sharp look.

"I do not."

Daisy enjoyed having a man to cook for and the midday meal was always well prepared and presented. Penelope asked Robert if he was eating well in Thames and he told her that he ate at the hotel where he lived and the food was adequate. He told them of the ships that arrived daily across the Gulf from Auckland and Sydney, and explained that the town was well stocked with both home-grown and imported foodstuffs.

His eyes often turned towards Billy sitting at the end of the table, nearly sixteen now, with his jaw squared up and grown tall and lean, much as Clem had been at the same age, with the same flop of blond hair. Robert watched his son feel across his plate, fingers lightly touching the surface of the food, nudging cuts of meat onto his fork. There was a hard set to Robert's face, a tightening of his lips, as if he couldn't bear to look at the sightless boy.

What did he see? Eloise wondered, as her father surveyed the family. He last knew Billy as a child, fever struck and sickly, but now his son was healthy and strong and entering manhood. Did he see that? What did he make of them all, did they bring him any joy at all?

Billy was happy to have his father home and tried to impress him. He told him of Serenity Wix and her rise to fame, now with her father in Waipukurau and together touring the preaching circuit. He couldn't see how Robert's interest waned. Billy, always the charmer, now couldn't pick up the cues. Sometimes it meant he had less social etiquette than Martha.

"Miss Wix has some alarming views, Father, you might not altogether approve of her anymore. She preaches on temperance and women's suffrage. She's very liberal. She has full crowds every service, they've had to move to a bigger hall to get the people in. She's been a good friend to us."

Robert regarded him without replying, as if genuinely surprised that a boy who couldn't see still had the ability to talk.

Billy persevered. "Do you have a good church in Thames? I'll bet you don't have a woman preacher!"

"No. No, we don't." Robert pushed his plate away. He went to his bag and brought out a bottle of wine, which he proceeded to open, and he filled a glass. Billy turned his head at the pull of the cork in the silent room.

Penelope asked, "Would you like us to provide wine with your dinner, Robert?"

His drinking in the past had always been in the privacy of his study. They had never had wine at the table.

"I will buy my own wine and drink with a meal if I choose. It's a habit of your brother's. American, no doubt."

He drank, not deeply. He wet and licked the liquid from his lips.

"Will you tell us, how is Horatio?"

But Robert wasn't forthcoming on that topic. "As I've already told you, your brother is well," was all he said.

A few weeks after his arrival, Robert called Eloise to him in the dining room, when the others were away about their tasks. He was sorting through a stack of papers and journals on the table but he stood up when she came in.

"Where's your mother?"

"In the garden, Father."

"I asked her to come, too. Fetch her, please."

He had a decisive look on his face. Eloise guessed what was coming. They were going to arrange her marriage to Cornelius. She had been waiting for the conversation and now it came to it, she supposed she should be happy.

She went through the kitchen and out to the vegetable patch where Martha and Penelope were tying beans. She supposed her parents had discussed her future and agreed it was time. It irked her that she had not been consulted by her mother. Never asked how she felt, whether she even liked Cornelius. It felt like a betrayal. Her mother's marriage, she had learned in an unguarded moment, had been arranged by her brother, who had, she said, "given her to Robert to look after along with the farm" when he had left England. Now Penelope was giving Eloise to Cornelius.

She realised, perhaps too late, that she should be surer of her feelings. All she knew was that she wasn't overwhelmingly glad. Was she such a romantic to feel she deserved a husband she loved? Once, she knew her father had hoped for better for her. Cornelius had no university education and he worked for a living. There were gentlemen in Cornwall who may have been her better match.

But they were far away and Cornelius was here, and she supposed she would grow used to being married to him. She didn't care that he worked hard. That was a point in his favour in the new country. An idle man was no use to anyone. At least she could have conversations with him about home and their shared memories.

When Eloise called, her mother put down her trowel, wiped her hands on her apron and obediently followed Eloise inside.

***

Robert was standing by the window, looking out with a scowl. He was snapping his fingers. It was an unexpected gesture and an ominous one, as if he was barely holding in his rage. He turned and glowered at them.

"Do you women think I am a fool?"

The mood in the room dropped like a stone into a deep pool.

Penelope's head lowered, but Eloise's chin shot up. She couldn't understand why her father would be angry. It was he who had accepted Cornelius and had invited him to join them. How did that make him a fool? She didn't understand how this meeting had got off to such a bad start. Her father's humour twisted like the wind.

The snapping stopped and the women stood in silence.

Robert snarled. "Do you think you can pull the wool over my eyes?" And then he shouted, "In my own *house?*"

And it suddenly dawned on Eloise that this meeting wasn't about her at all. Penelope stood with her hands clasped and her head down. She obviously knew exactly why they were there, in this room, having this confrontation.

"Whose baby is it?" he asked, the threatening note in his voice an unsheathed knife.

Of course he would have found out. It was no secret in Napier that the child was Martha's. The only reason they weren't shunned in the streets was because they were under Serenity's protection. Oh, but she should have told him! Here she had been fretting about Cornelius when she should have been finding a road to safety for Martha and Winnie. She should have taken it upon herself to write to her father before Winnie was born and tell him everything. Whatever he would have done then, this was far, far worse.

"Who is the baby's father?"

Eloise wanted to say she didn't know. But she did know. She found she couldn't lie to her father. "He is the son of the wagoner. Martha didn't understand that what they did was wrong."

"How was this possible?"

Eloise opened her mouth to speak but Robert cut across her. "I'm not talking to you, Eloise. I'm talking to my *wife*. How was it possible that a wagoner's son had access to my daughter?"

Penelope spoke quietly and clearly, looking forwards at a spot on Robert's waistcoat. "I sent the girls south with a wagon train to Norsewood. There was news of an English sailor on one of the Norwegian ships. We thought it might be Matthew."

Robert took a step closer to them. Eloise was astounded that her mother still had not shared the news of their journey to the Norwegian camp with him.

"You thought a sailor might be Matthew? And was he?"

"No." Penelope offered nothing more. Eloise wondered at her self-control;

there was so much more to tell. But her mother's habit of silence was profound.

Robert shook his head in disbelief. "Why wasn't I told of this?"

"You weren't here, Robert."

"And while the girls were off chasing sailors, Martha was rutting with the wagoner's son. How about you, Eloise? Were you also debasing yourself in the back of a cart?"

"No, Father."

"What is his name, this wagon driver?"

"I don't remember."

"Oh, I think you probably do." He stepped forwards so he was inches from her face, and as he spoke she saw red flecks in the whites of his eyes, a glittering cruelty. "What is his name?"

Eloise shook her head miserably.

"You will tell me his name, Eloise, or I will whip it out of your pitiful sister."

"McCreedy."

"And why did you lie to me? Why did you tell me Martha was looking after an orphan? You had me believe she was doing charitable work. How dare you lie to me!"

"I am sorry. Of course we should have told you immediately. I am so sorry, Father. It was my fault. It was wrong."

"It should never have happened! Martha is an imbecile and cannot be left alone!" He swung to confront Penelope. "Your only job is to look after my children. How could you not protect her?" The accusation, with all its implications, flew from him. "So. It is done. Your daughter has given birth to a bastard half-breed and brought him into my house."

He turned his back on them and paced across the room, muttering, "I have five children and four of them, four of my children, have fallen beyond repair. God, your retribution is cruel."

"The baby is a girl." Penelope lifted her head and spoke uncowed.

It was like a sharp lick of lightning and Eloise waited for the thunder to hit.

"What did you say, Penelope?"

"You said 'him'. But the baby is a girl and her name is Winifred. Martha and I named her after my grandmother."

Eloise felt a cold wind blowing under the door, through the open window, curling around the room, slipping into cuts in her skin.

"The baby is nobody and will go to an orphanage."

"No, she won't."

"No?"

"No, Robert. There will be no talk of orphanages, or of sending the baby away. We cannot choose which of our children come and which go. Martha's baby is ours, we will accept her and baptise her and we will care for her. God has given Winifred to us and I swear, as God is my witness, I will protect her with my life."

For a second, Eloise thought her father was going to dash the back of his hand across her mother's face. His elbow came forwards and his hand drew back and the threat of violence rolled across his face. But he didn't strike her. He clenched his fist, fighting against himself. In the face of this upright and honest woman, he lowered his hand, still clenched, to his side.

"Matthew is dead, you know," he said savagely.

Eloise's hands flew up to cover her mouth to prevent herself from crying out. How fast this storm of words was raging, tearing the fabric of her family to shreds.

Penelope was still staring at her husband defiantly. She didn't flicker.

"As surely as is Clem. Don't tell me that God has taken my sons and given me this thing in compensation."

But Penelope didn't say anything. She stood face to face with her husband and stared him down, a woman protecting her grandchild. Eloise had never seen her look so strong.

Eventually, it was Robert who gave way. He closed his eyes and screwed up his face and when he opened them again Eloise thought his look was pleading – as if he had fallen and was asking Penelope to help him back up. As his chin fell, Penelope's lifted.

Robert pushed past her and left the room, banging the door in his rage behind him.

Eloise helped her mother as she collapsed into a chair. She was quivering like a leaf in the wind.

***

They didn't see Robert for nearly a week and Eloise languished in powerless limbo. Finally, with her mother's approval, she left a letter for him at his club. She made no mention of Martha or the baby, but told him of Mr Friberg's assumption that Matthew went ashore at Cape Verde and was making his way back to England.

There is hope, she wrote. *He will write to us.*

Still, Robert didn't return.

On Saturday, Serenity came to visit with her father, who had joined his now considerably more popular daughter on the preaching circuit. He was stiff and formal; perhaps the visit to the Sansonnet family was against his wishes. His mission in Waipukurau was struggling and he appeared tired and unwell. But to his credit, he was proud of his daughter and accompanied her with good grace, stepping out of the limelight as she evangelised.

They stayed for tea, and Eloise told them of the confrontation with Robert. The party watched the door uncomfortably, knowing he could reappear at any time. Mr Wix grew more and more uneasy. He told them he heard that Robert had made enquiries at the Mission for an orphanage. "But the Catholics told him that there is no need for an orphanage in Hawke's Bay. All children are loved."

"I wish that were true," said Serenity, with feeling.

"We have such needs in this heathen country. I see it in my parish. The Māori are primitive souls and I try to bring them to God but their morals are lax. There are half-breed babies on their Marae and on the farms and, I am ashamed to say, sin has entered a Christian mission. Martha is a simpleton and an innocent. I understand this. A man took advantage of her. But there are women who go willingly into sin and I despair that the work we do here falls on deaf ears. If a woman will not admit her depravity how can she find redemption?" He rubbed his temples. "Maybe Robert is right to look for an orphanage for the baby. How can Martha be saved from her sin when she has the baby here on her knee?" Mr Wix had long since stopped trying to make any connection with Martha, and spoke now as if she wasn't sitting at the table beside him. Eloise wished her sister would hold her head up and look at him, talk back to him, let him know she was neither simple nor Godless. But Martha, as usual, let the conversation go past her.

"I know a family in Waipukurau who lost a child and are unable to have another. They are desperate for a baby. A girl would do."

Penelope spoke up. "No, Mr Wix. We are firm on this. Winnie stays with us."

The minister began to protest, but Serenity interrupted. "If that is your decision, Mrs Sansonnet, then I am glad. The child will be raised in love and with God." She smiled at Martha and the baby in her arms. The girl's fat little hands reached out to touch Martha's face, and Martha returned her look without much expression. When the kitchen door opened, though, she sprang up from her seat, arms wrapped protectively around her bundle.

It was Daisy, come through to draw the curtains.

Serenity and her father left before dark.

"Give Mr Sansonnet our best regards on his return. And Mrs Sansonnet, know this," the minister said sternly. "I would prefer that you send the child away. However, if your decision is to keep it, and you are supported by my daughter in this decision, then I would like to be the one to baptise her and bring her into the church. I will speak to Mr Sansonnet."

But Penelope appeared not to hear him, her eyes on the door, the twitch of a muscle playing on her jaw.

Eloise spoke for her. "Thank you indeed, Mr Wix."

Robert reappeared the following afternoon as they were clearing the dinner table.

"Leave me some of that," he said to Daisy, and he took a plate from her and a slice of the loaf and off-cuts of mutton. "Wait, please," he said to

Penelope as she prepared to leave the room.

The family sat back down and waited in silence while Robert ate. He paid them no attention but Eloise felt he was very aware of them, watching to see who would stand up to him next. Eventually, he placed his elbows on the table and pointed his finger at Penelope.

"The baby can stay," he said gruffly. "You, Penelope, can adopt it. Call it a Brooke if you must, but it will never be a Sansonnet. Martha's disgrace will not mean disgrace for the whole family. It must not affect Eloise's prospects. My last hope!" He picked a piece of meat from his teeth and sat back in his chair. "Where is Cornelius Wainwright? I wrote to him to meet me here."

Once again, Eloise was bewildered by the lack of communication between her mother and father. Her mother had not told him.

"Cornelius went to find you," Eloise said. "He left the day we received your letter saying you were coming home. If you wrote to him in the same post, he won't have received it."

"What are you saying? He's gone where?"

"Oh, Father! Cornelius has been here nearly eight months and says he has written to you about his intentions many times with no reply. He wants your permission to court me. He doesn't know if we are engaged or not – the poor man is as confused as we all are!"

"I asked you where he is."

"He went to Thames on the steamer."

"When?" There was panic in his voice.

They were interrupted by a sharp rap on the front door.

"Who's that?" demanded Robert.

Eloise stood up. "It may be Mr Wix, though we are not expecting them back today. I will go."

If it was the minister, he had not picked a good time to return. Her father had never been one to sit quietly while a preacher told him how to behave, and now their battle was won Mr Wix would likely make it worse. She needed to find a way to deflect him.

But when she opened the front door, it wasn't the minister.

***

Cornelius Wainwright stood on the doorstep with his hand poised as if to knock again, so it appeared he was about to hit Eloise in the nose.

It was such a relief to see him there, decent and reliable. His expression was confused and his knuckles were poised to strike, but Eloise recognised the face of a good man. He would be her ally. Perhaps, when they were married, Martha and Winnie could live with them, and the baby would be out of her father's house and safe. She almost laughed as he lifted his raised hand to straighten his hat, as if that had been his intention all along.

He pulled a formal expression down over his face.

"Miss Sansonnet."

"Oh, Cornelius, do come in! We were talking about you. I am so pleased to see you back! You missed Father in Thames, but he is here now and you can talk to him directly."

She reached out a hand to him but, surprisingly, he didn't take it. He firmly hooked his hands onto his coat lapels. He looked as though he were pushing his nerves back down under his coat.

"It is your father I have come to see."

"Yes, yes, I know you have. It has all been very confusing but you can talk to Father now and sort everything out."

Seeing that he was being extremely formal and was definitely not going to take her hand, Eloise let it go and withdrew so he could pass into the house without touching her. She took his hat and his coat and ushered him into the drawing room, slightly quizzical at his solemn expression.

"Will you wait here while I fetch Father?" she said, and he nodded.

For a second, she wanted to ruffle him, to put him off balance and knock the pompous expression away. The door to the dining room was closed, there was no one looking through the window. If she was going to marry this man, he had to loosen up a bit when the two of them were alone. On impulse she stepped forwards suddenly, put one hand on his chest and reached up to kiss him on his rather soft, full lips.

It was like she had stuck a dagger in him.

He jolted back, horrified, shaking his head as he wiped away her kiss with the back of his hand. He stared at her ferociously.

"How dare you!"

Eloise, aghast, stood flat-footed, a burning flush running up from her chest and blooming across her neck. She felt pins behind her eyes, a sharp stab to open the tear ducts.

She stumbled back in confusion, lifelong training folding her into an obedient half curtsy as he backed away.

The door behind her opened and Robert came in.

Through her tears, Eloise instantly saw that something was horribly wrong.

Cornelius stood with his feet firmly planted and his shoulders drawn right back to push his chest forwards in an extraordinarily aggressive way. It was so unlike his usual, deferential manner around Robert. He glared at the older man with something like a sneer, but nastier – a wipe of disgust smudged across his expression.

Robert was reduced, crumpled almost, his arrogance melted into his boots. He was old and weary, unable to stand up to the young challenger. Young Cornelius.

The scene was bizarre.

Behind Robert came Martha, Billy and Penelope with the baby in her arms, awake now, eyes wide and witnessing.

Cornelius stood his ground and confronted the older man.

"Robert Sansonnet, I accuse you." Unlike his strong stance, his voice was high pitched and emotional. "I accuse you of foul and immoral practices. I have been to Thames and I have learned exactly what your business is. You have a partnership with Horatio Brooke and I know about him, too. I know his past and why he left England, chased out for the seduction of a young virgin. He boasted to me of this! And yet you came here to form an alliance with him and told me we would be farming! I accuse you! Your business, with your partner Horatio Brooke, keeps young women in shame. Your business is a brothel." Cornelius spat the word.

He waved his hand around the drawing room, encompassing the whole house and the family within it. "All of this wealth is a sham, created on the earnings of sin. You, sir, are a wicked man. You are a disgrace to this house and your family and I ... and I denounce you!"

Bright spots appeared on Cornelius's cheeks as he took a deep breath. His face twisted in pain. His misery was inescapable.

His words dropped like stones into Eloise. A brothel? She felt the gorge rising in her throat. Her father ran a brothel?

"You brought me across the world with lies and half-truths. And you, Eloise!" He turned to her, leading still with his puffed chest as if it were keeping him afloat. "You led me on and tempted me and tried to make love to me and all the while you, too, were full of lies. I know the baby isn't an orphan, look at the way Mrs Sansonnet holds her grandchild! The child is yours, Eloise! Is that not so? Your child with your handsome furniture maker who comes to the door with a *rocking* chair for you and the baby? I saw the man, I saw the *disappointment* when he found me in your house. I saw how you cried when you ran after him. I've heard about the taint of scandal that lives within these walls."

"That is enough, Cornelius," said Penelope. She stepped forwards and Cornelius, for the first time, really looked at the uncovered child in her arms. The wispy black hair and rich brown eyes, the burnished skin. The baby was no Norwegian. Cornelius's expression of disgust turned to shock and he buckled, the floor unsteady under his feet.

But his chest re-filled and he said what he had come to say. "I want no part of this family. You are twisted and immoral and in your company my good name is stained. My association with you, from this day forwards, is over. We are not family. We do not know each other."

He staggered back against the side table in his haste to leave and knocked a jug of flowers. It teetered and then fell on the floorboards, the water splashing over his shoes. He bent to pick it up as politeness demanded when things fall, as he had done many times in Cornwall, clumsily apologising for something dropped, something broken. But he steadied himself against the door frame, stepped over the flowers and was gone.

After a moment of numbness, Penelope handed the wriggling baby to Martha and turned to her husband, who, eventually, lifted his head to meet her eyes. Eloise saw her mother, straight-shouldered, was not so much smaller than her cowed husband. He had always appeared to tower over her.

His expression was that of a defeated man.

"Robert," she said, her voice low and even. "Is what Cornelius says the truth? Is this your business that has taken you away all these months, and that brings this sudden income into my household? Do you keep a brothel?"

Eloise waited for the denial, but it didn't come.

Robert nodded once. "It is true."

"Is it also true that my brother violated a woman and this is why he left England?"

"This is also true. Montclair's sister. Montclair would kill him if he returned."

"You never thought to tell me this?"

"No."

It was a reckoning that held them like mud, slow moving and slow thinking. These were words to think over later, to understand. Penelope hadn't finished.

"Perhaps this is also the time for you to tell me the whole story. Why your father would have nothing to do with you. Why, all those years ago, you came to stay with my brother?"

Robert nodded, but appeared incapable of working his words out. His face was drowned in shame.

Penelope kept on. "Horatio told me you were stood down from university before you were sent away. Perhaps you will tell me why."

"I seduced a girl. She was just a serving girl."

"Is there more?"

His eyes dropped away into the corner of the room. "She took..." He played with some words in his mouth, but didn't let them out. "She couldn't live with the shame," he said eventually.

There were years that ran in sequence behind Penelope's eyes then. Eloise watched her go back and back and saw a look of repugnance grow on her mother's face as she measured her life with this man, her husband, with whom she had lived for twenty-five years while he carried sins that must have flowed from him like tainted blood.

Eventually, her father moved and broke away. He walked past them. He took his hat from the sideboard and his coat from the stand in the hall. He shrugged his arms into the sleeves. He cast a backwards glance into the room as if to plaster the image of his family to his mind. And then he left.

On the doorstep they heard a scuffle and Robert shouted, "Who the devil are you? Get out of my way!"

There was the thud of someone being pushed aside, and then they heard Robert's heavy tread leave the verandah and march off up the road.

Sickened and appalled, Eloise sank down onto the sofa, unable to look at her mother. She reached up a hand for Billy to steady him, and guided him next to her where he sat, holding her hand and staring into the room, the blind boy seeing the tension, thick as syrup, as well as any of them.

Penelope stayed standing, her shoulders set strongly but her countenance fragile, a glass dropped from a height waiting to hit the stone floor.

It was Martha who saw what no one else saw, beyond them to where a man now stood in the doorway. Martha, who had stood with her expressionless face during the whole altercation with Cornelius and her father, whose countenance rarely showed any of the feelings she experienced, who now, Eloise saw, smiled shyly. A version of Martha that Eloise had rarely seen was walking across the room to the young Māori man who was rubbing his shoulder where Robert had pushed him against the wall.

His hair was cropped short and he was dressed in a white open-necked, pressed cotton shirt and a soft black suit slightly too big for him. He had filled out, his shoulders broad and straight and the angles of his face more manly, but it was Hemi who stood on their doorstep, and he was smiling right back at Martha. Eloise saw in his face a kindness and a shyness that moved her with such a lurch she felt pain in her throat as she realised that this, then, was what love looked like.

Martha took the baby to him and Hemi gazed in wonder down at the sleeping Winnie in her arms.

"My father told me you had our baby, Martha," he said, almost in a whisper. "I came straight away."

CHAPTER TEN

Penelope walked out of the house with the remains of her family the morning after Robert left, onto rain-washed streets, locking the door and leaving the key behind for Mr Duffy. Before they left, she gathered her children in the drawing room, without sitting, and apologised to them. She had failed them and the family had been brought down. She said it defiantly, in such a sure voice that Eloise had the peculiar feeling that the opposite was true, that this wasn't failure at all, but progress. She made them pack no more than they could carry, and only things they had brought with them from Cornwall.

"We will not come back here," said Penelope. "Take what you need in your journey bags. Nothing purchased in the last year."

Eloise quickly pushed her old sea boots and some clothes into a bag and threw it by the door. Then she went back for her chair. She couldn't lift it alone, but with Billy she carried it step by careful step down the stairs, and lifted it onto the back porch, under cover of a blanket.

With nowhere to go, they accepted Hemi's proposal to put up in the vacant storage room above the wagon yard.

Hemi's father, Mr McCreedy, had a room below. But when the family arrived in the yards, straggling in through the summer rain with their possessions and their uncertainties, the man was not the boisterous and energetic figure Eloise remembered from her journey. Here was a pitiful man, bruised and broken.

Robert had visited him the week before. He had come at night with his accusations and his violence and his heavy fists. Mr McCreedy thought himself lucky to be alive. Robert had smashed his knees with a stick. The bone setter had made him a crude splint and crutches.

"He has a nasty temper, your man," Mr McCreedy said to Penelope, when Hemi directed her and her burdens through the yard. The man's rugged face was bruised, his eye was blackened and the hand holding the crutch had bandaged fingers. "He was after my son, but I saw the murder in his eyes and I swore to him my son was drowned. Which is the truth, mind, my wife and first son together, drowned they were, in the lagoon, long ago. And I'm truly sorry for you, ma'am. The damage he done me will heal, but I daresay he has brought you down further than he could ever knock me. That space upstairs is nothing like you are used to, but it is large and dry and it is safe. There's no one gets up there but past me and I'm not moving from my place here, by the stairs."

There was a narrow wooden staircase that led from the back of the yard to the floor above, and at the foot Hemi had set up a day bed for his father from which he could work and rest. There was a desk with his work books and a lamp and, clear in view on the table, a revolver.

"You won't be needing that. He won't come for us," Penelope said with conviction. "I don't imagine we will see him again."

Eloise sent Hemi to fetch her rocking chair from the back porch of the house.

He left immediately, willingly, and brought it back carefully slung in the blanket, making light of the weight. He carried it up the stairs to the attic and set it by the one small window overlooking the yard.

"It's from Lars, eh?"

She nodded. Hemi knew. He had been there with them at Te Whiti and he was no fool. He had seen two people, not a gentleman's daughter and a labourer. Just two people, a man and a woman.

"You ever see him again?" he asked her.

"No, not since Te Whiti." And it suddenly occurred to her, her heart jumping. "Have you seen him? On your travels?"

But Hemi hadn't. He didn't do the Seventy Mile Bush run anymore and the Scandinavians kept to themselves, a tight little community. The town was growing, he told her, Norsewood. The road was finished, but the railway line had stalled and was being redirected another way. It was a hard life in the bush. Hemi shook his head with respect. "Never seen anyone work as hard as the Scandis. The English people, you know, they sit on horses and talk and point their hands, but those Scandi fellas, they take their jackets off and get busy. They cut down trees so fast. So much of the bush has gone now. It's all chopped, or burned away."

He sounded sad.

"That's good progress. Don't you think?"

He shrugged. "Do you know who planted those trees?"

"No. Do you?"

"Nah. That's the point. Maybe it was Tāne Mahuta. Maybe it was God." Hemi sighed. "I don't like to go there anymore. I don't recognise it."

Eloise sat in her chair and rocked to the rhythm of Lars and his brothers swinging axes in the trees. The bush was so vast, and so empty of people. She loved the idea of a road stretching through it like a river, connecting clearings where families lived with their animals. It made the place less wild, more civilised. But it was an interesting question from Hemi. Who had planted the trees?

Their meagre possessions lay in a couple of neat piles in the long, dusty room. The place had been a warehouse of sorts, there were boxes and bolts of cloth and broken bits of saddlery, an old broom. So this, now, was home. How far from home they had come. How stripped. And yet.

Her mother picked up the broom and began sweeping bits of debris from the floor, with a vitality that had been missing from her spirit for so long.

Is this what you do when your life crumbles? wondered Eloise. Sweep?

Hemi found them bedrolls and he nailed some canvas across the attic beams to divide the space, and from the yard he brought a large shallow box with a blanket for the baby. His baby. His eyes sought Winnie and he smiled his wide-toothed grin at her. He filled jugs of water from the rain barrel and brought bread and a pot of stew from the chop shop. From somewhere he borrowed an oil lamp and matches. He staggered up the stairs with crates and boxes, making Billy hold the ends and guiding him around the corners, talking to him all the time, and from the crates

Penelope made a rudimentary table and bench.

Eloise watched it all from behind a curtain in her mind. A fine gauze had wrapped itself around her head and trapped her inside; she could see and hear, but she felt like a ghost. Otherworldly.

She rocked and traced the carvings of her chair and felt comfort through her fingertips. She didn't need to close her eyes to feel loved. Through the wood she simply absorbed it. Slowly, the mist cleared and her strength began to return. Eventually, she unfolded herself from the chair, found a rag and started cleaning the glass in the filthy window to let in the light. It was something.

It was late in the evening when Hemi made a final trip up the stairs, to check they were settled and needed nothing more for the night.

Eloise had taken the baby off Martha. Martha was having a turn and her anxiety was upsetting Winnie, so Eloise sat with the baby in the chair and rocked her, her fractious crying quietening slowly. Martha had managed the move well and had been stoic while the new room was set up around her. But in the end there were too many changes and too much tension, and she sat now on a mattress in the corner with her back to the wall and her arms wrapped around her legs, and she tap tapped with her feet, rocking back and forwards. They let her be.

But Hemi ignored their lead and went across the room to her. She appeared not to see him. He sat down next to her and laid his arm, with his hand up, along the mattress between them. He was still as a bolster, warm blooded.

When Winnie finally slept, Eloise rocked smoothly forwards and off the chair and transferred the baby to the makeshift crib. Billy was asleep at the top of the stairs and Penelope was sitting on a box, eyes wide and dreaming.

Eloise nudged her and pointed to the corner. Hemi hadn't moved, but Martha was asleep with her head dropped on his shoulder, and her small hand was holding his upturned one.

Penelope sighed. She said quietly, "I have been wrong about so many things."

A week later, Hemi and Martha took a carriage to Clive and were married by Mr Wix in the sight of God.

Eloise held baby Winnie during her parents' wedding and Serenity Wix gave the blessing.

"Can a blind boy be a witness?" asked Billy, but he was smiling as Hemi put the pen into his hand and guided him to put his signature in the register.

***

Hemi took over the running of the business while Mr McCreedy recovered from the savage beating Robert had inflicted on him. The splint had broken and had to be replaced, the leg mended slowly and Mr McCreedy, an impatient man, found it difficult to lie still. A young yard worker called Taffy was commandeered to push Mr McCreedy around in a wheeled chair as he went about his business in the yard, but the strain formed a permanent grimace on the old man's face and he was grey when Eloise brought him dinner in the evening.

Hemi went away with the wagons on the weekly trip to Waipukurau, where they changed horses at the hotel and returned two days later, bringing produce and passengers from the farms in the south. Martha remained with the family in their attic above the yard but she walked out with Hemi whenever he was home, pushing the baby in a cart that Mr McCreedy had one of his men make up. It was a large, ugly thing like a small wagon, but it rolled smoothly over the rough streets and the baby didn't mind. Martha was fortunate she didn't notice the way people turned away when they saw her with her Māori husband. Because she didn't recognise disapproving looks, they couldn't upset her.

Her baby's crib was, with the rest of their belongings, discarded in Robert Sansonnet's house and they closed that door in their minds and never went that way, towards the hill.

All except Martha. She had been told not to go back into the house and took the instruction literally. No one had explicitly forbidden the garden. So she went back and harvested the crops and took a garden spade to dig up everything they had planted. She made Hemi haul it back to the yard in a large handcart.

"What are you going to do with all that greenery and dirt?" roared Mr McCreedy. "Here, give us the vegetables but get rid of the rest of that muck. This is a working yard, not a market garden or a bloody hostel. God damn you, boy, you are testing me. Get rid of it!"

"She needs it." Hemi stepped back so Mr McCreedy didn't run over his feet in his chair. "She likes gardening. It makes her peaceful."

"We've got two teams of eight to make up tomorrow, going up to Kuripapango. I'll not have the men and horses getting tangled up in your flowering beans. Go on, boy, throw it over the fence somewhere and get back to work."

"She needs a patch of garden."

"Take it down to old widow Povey, then. She was starting to put a garden down when the old boy died. Got no one to help her now. Throw that stuff down there. She'll be grateful. She might make me a pie if you say it's from me. Tell her it's a gift from me. Go on with you!"

And so Hemi and Martha took the cart with half the garden overflowing the sides down to the big house near the river, and offered their services to the elderly woman. On his days at home, Hemi dug her vegetable beds and Martha planted and Penelope allowed herself to be coaxed out of doors and went with Martha to the old woman's house. Once the vegetables were in, they began to restore the borders and the flower beds. Despite their fall and the family disgrace, Eloise thought her mother was better. Happier. Healthier. Sometimes, she and the widow Povey walked in her garden and talked about England. Penelope had a friend at last, someone who had never known her husband.

Winnie crawled about in the earth and grew fat. Her first steps were on the rough grass of the garden by the river.

As Mr McCreedy predicted, Mrs Povey did make them pies, from vegetables and dripping, which they brought home to share, but the long autumn ended with weeks of rain and as winter drew in Penelope and Martha stayed indoors, leaving the garden to the cold and winter floods. In the room above the yard Penelope took in some occasional mending for the widow, her neat stitches a skill coming back from childhood. Martha did nothing more than watch Winnie tottering about her feet. She waited for Hemi to return from his trips, bringing warmth and a breath of happiness.

Eloise did what she could over the winter. She took Billy to the church hall and waited through his piano lesson with Miss Belle, and left him to accompany old Mr Belle when he went out tuning pianos. Eloise explained that they could not pay for lessons or anything towards the informal apprenticeship Billy received, but Miss Belle insisted Billy was her project and she was pleased to help. Billy grumbled and Eloise felt shamed, but without charity they had nothing. She was learning to live with shame. She had no friend other than Serenity and they relied entirely on the wagoner and Hemi for their food and lodging, such as it was.

"Why does he feed us?" she asked her mother as they walked in the rain to the lagoon. Mr McCreedy had given them money to buy eels from the Māori who gathered at the riverside, selling kaimoana from their canoes. The eels' long muscular bodies twisted and writhed, alive on the spears. Eloise had never eaten eel and the idea made her feel queasy, but Mr McCreedy had laughed at her and said an eel was just what she needed. "I don't understand why he puts up with us. Especially as Father nearly killed him. Why does he let us stay?"

The rain was through her cotton bonnet now and she felt its chill on her scalp. She wrapped her hands in the cloth bag she carried to bring the eels home.

"He feels Winnie is his responsibility. And so she is."

"And us?"

"Oh, Eloise, where else would we go? He is rough and coarse, but Mr McCreedy is not a bad man. I don't want to be pitied by anyone, but he pities us and we must bear it. We must make ourselves useful to him, and stay quiet and out of his way."

"I don't want to be in debt to him."

Her mother shook her head sympathetically.

"You are a woman. You will always be in debt to somebody."

"Serenity thinks women should have jobs, and earn money themselves."

"I have heard you two talking. What sort of job would you like?"

"I could run the bank, like Mr Duffy."

"And meet all day with men asking questions about their money?"

"Or a doctor. It wouldn't be hard to be a better doctor than Doctor Croft. Winnie is a better doctor than Doctor Croft."

"You could be a teacher. There are plenty of women teachers."

"I couldn't!"

"Why don't you ask at Napier Boys' School?"

Eloise knew she couldn't go to any school in Napier and ask to be a teacher. She tried to protect her mother from her reception in the town, but Napier was a small place, and just one or two enquiries would reveal the status of her family. Living in a yard, an abandoned family with a mixed-race marriage and the scandal of an illegitimate child. No one would employ her. Some of the shopkeepers were reluctant to serve her, and she had never been invited anywhere other than with Serenity or Miss Belle. She was barely brave enough to go to church. It was as well her mother was protected from it.

The Māori waved their speared eels as Eloise and Penelope approached. They sat under a shelter made of leaves that the rain came through, their canoes pulled up on the mud of the riverbank, waiting for trade.

To Eloise's surprise, her shy mother took the lead and approached the men, pointing to the eels and holding out a coin.

Up close, the things were thick and nasty looking, slippery with blood and brine.

"You want skinned?"

"Oh, yes. Yes, skinned if you would. Two, please."

He picked up a sharp knife and split an eel free from the spear. The long slimy thing lunged in his hand and he held it, wriggling, towards Eloise, who leaped back from the ugly, half-dead fish. The men laughed and pointed, amused by the novelty of her. The Māori put the knife through the head to kill it, and then, while it was still twitching, he ran the blade around the skin behind the gills, tucked his fingers in and pulled the skin back like Eloise would pull off a stocking.

With swift dexterity, he gutted and filleted the eels and put the pieces into Penelope's proffered sacking bag.

"Heads no good," he said, and threw the remains of the fish out into the water.

Both the women's faces pursed into a grimace, but Penelope took the bag and paid him.

"Here," the man said, grabbing a bunch of green leaves from inside his canoe and adding them to the bag. "Rangiora. Wrap around eel and put on fire. Good good!"

Penelope took one of the leaves and stroked it. One side repelled the water and was a slippery, waxy green; the other a soft white cloth of fine, velvet matted hairs.

The men were laughing as they walked away. When they were out of earshot, Eloise took her mother's arm and said, "Do you know what's making them laugh? It's the way you are stroking that plant."

"These leaves? He called them rangiora."

"Yes, well, there is another name for them. Hemi taught the Norwegians on the trail. See the back?" She rubbed the soft underside. "They call it Bushman's Friend. What do you think they use that for, out in the bush?"

"Oh!"

And despite the rain, and the helplessness of their situation and the fact that they had a bag of slimy eel they had to turn, somehow, into dinner, the women laughed, little stitches knitting them back together.

Later that night, when the others were sleeping and Eloise sat in her chair with her fingers, as always, tracing the carvings of the bush and leaves, Penelope came and pulled up a box and sat next to her, looking at her daughter's far away face.

"Tell me about the chair, Eloise."

And Eloise, tired of keeping Lars secret in her heart, told her mother the story of the boy she met on the ship and fell in love with in the heart of the Seventy Mile Bush.

***

Business hardly slowed over the winter, the wagons ordered frequently into the hills not only south but west towards Kuripapango, where farmers were opening up the interior. Hemi was mostly away, Mr McCreedy driving him to work harder and turn around the loads faster. He was a relentless taskmaster and spent long hours on his unsteady feet, waving his crutch, directing operations and hobbling around the yard on his crippled leg. When there were no wagons in the yard he checked and mended his tack and met with settlers and the freight companies, doing deals on a spit and a handshake with his habitual crude banter. He bought out the neighbouring blacksmith and expanded the stables, he employed a harness maker and had samples of leathers from the tanners spread all across his workshop.

The attic room was cold and the Sansonnets went about their work wrapped in blankets. They washed and cooked, in a primitive way, for Mr McCreedy, and made rag rugs for the floor. The fumes from the tannery and the stables rose, a clammy, cold vapour that seeped through the floorboards and permeated their lives, and the cockroaches climbed the walls and lived with them above the yard, but Penelope would hear no complaint. "It is no sin to be poor," she said.

Eloise took Billy to Miss Belle each Sunday, who accompanied him to church to play for the service. Sometimes Eloise took a place in the back pew, but the good people of Napier avoided her and the minister was a dispiriting preacher, with none of Serenity's kindness. She left the service feeling downtrodden rather than uplifted. The only one to greet her was Mrs Duffy and though she meant well, Eloise cringed at her pious pity.

Billy came home one Sunday with a message from Mr Duffy. It seemed Billy had been promoted in the banker's estimation to the head of the household. Eloise heard his voice settling into its new low register and thought how far down the pecking order he had been just two years before.

"He has news of Father," Billy told them as he came up the stairs. "Or lack of news, more to the point."

"I don't know your father," Penelope told him.

"Your brother has been trying to contact you."

"I have no brother."

"Then I shall give you news of two unknown men, Mother. It's a strange story. Father never arrived back in Thames. Uncle Horatio thought perhaps he had gone to Auckland. But there was no word. Then a couple of months ago our uncle met the master of the ship that had carried Father from Napier. The master remembered him, said he was terribly seasick and angry, and began fighting with the crew. They put him ashore on a muddy riverbank near a place called Wairoa."

"What's at Wairoa?" asked Eloise.

"Nothing. It has the remnants of a military base and a small trading post; there's been no proper town there since the war. Uncle Horatio sent someone to trace Father. A Wairoa farmer remembered a man was put ashore from the ship and asked him for the road to Thames. The man stole his boots and some provisions and wasn't seen again."

"How long is the road from Wairoa to Thames?"

"That's the thing," said Billy, "there isn't a road. There is an old military track that leads to the Urewera mountains. They're impassable. He went into the bush and never came back."

Eloise had put her father aside. There had been no mention of him for months. The family had gone on as if life had always been so, as if their memories started in the room above the yard. They had uncoupled from the strong family who used to live on a farm in Cornwall and pulled their horizons in within the four walls. This father, who had betrayed them so shamefully and then walked away, was a man Eloise didn't know. But she remembered another man. She remembered the father from her happy childhood. She remembered the delight on his handsome face as she perched on her first pony and held out her hands for him to keep her steady. His pride when she had memorised a Christmas poem and recited it to the family; she couldn't have been more than four or five but the love on his face had stayed with her. She remembered frightening him in Tintagel when he thought she had tumbled off the cliff and how he had fallen to the ground in relief when she had sprung up from behind a boulder. "I thought I had lost you, Princess!" he had said, then. Back then.

Now he had left them.

Eloise wouldn't cry in front of her mother, who was steadfast and determined to be brave. But at night she cried, muffled and alone.

She went out walking, on her own, and found she didn't care that the women of Napier tutted and men called to her as she passed. They were nothing to do with her. She walked south down the new road to Taradale and looked up at the Mission on the hill. She thought of Cornelius sometimes, of how he had turned his back on them. She was guilty of hiding Martha's condition from him and was sorry for that now. A lie was a sin and she determined not to lie again. She would be herself. She was nobody's princess.

The Napier to Hastings railway opened, and trains rattled and puffed past Mr McCreedy's yard. Once Eloise followed the track between the railway and the sea, the rhythm of her boots a percussion with the crash of the waves and the birds soaring overhead, but no trains went past and she walked all the way to the station at Clive, running between the tracks across the bridges. It wasn't until she turned for home that she remembered Buttercup.

The farmer was surprised to see Eloise walking through his paddocks alone. "We thought you'd gone away, Miss Sansonnet! We wrote to you several times. Your Buttercup is with foal again. We'll do the same arrangement, shall we, sell the foal to pay for her keep?"

"May I see her?"

They walked out across the planted fields, green with winter wheat. It was as warm as summer.

"We've had no frosts this winter," the farmer told her. "Been a bit boggy, with the rain in October, but we've had good vegetables all the year. You're a Cornish lass, do you remember the winters there? Chilblains, I used to get, something shocking, but we've been here twelve years now and not been bothered by them at all. Here she is now, here's your girl."

Buttercup came with memories of better days. She leaned her long nose down against Eloise's cheek and blew a deep, shuddering breath of warm air that blasted down her neck into her coat, tickling Eloise, making her both smile and cry.

"I can't help noticing the state of your boots, Miss Sansonnet. I hope you've not fallen on hard times. I take it your father is back home with you now?"

There was a hedge of flax running along the side of the field and Eloise noticed a flutter of birds. They were sleek and black.

"Father? No. Father is no longer with us. But my sister married, and we stay with her husband's family."

"I'm sorry to hear that. Is it–"

"Are they starlings? I think they are!"

Their attention turned to the birds, swaying along tall spears protruding from the glossy flax. They were energetic, dipping their heads into the dull red flower tubes, hopping from bush to bush. "We brought them on the ship with us," Eloise told him. "We thought they had flown away, that we'd never see them again."

"Starlings, that's right. We're pleased to have them; we had such a plague of caterpillars in the kitchen gardens over the years. These are nesting in the barn; they make a right feed of all the crawlies. I'm not so happy with them in the orchard, mind. They're over at the Mission, too, eating up the grapes."

"Martha will be so happy!" said Eloise, and she kissed Buttercup on her soft nose and said goodbye to the farmer, who stood scratching his head as she ran off back to the railway line.

"Can I take you to town on the horse, Miss Sansonnet?" he called after her, but she turned and waved.

"I'm fine, Mr Rowe. Really, I will be fine."

***

Like every winter, this one passed, and the light began to linger longer in the evenings.

One night, when the spring growth had begun and the mud on the stones was hidden beneath a fresh cover of green slime, Mr McCreedy slipped and his leg snapped back again on the old break. He lay at the far end of the yard for a night in the rain, calling pitifully, until Eloise found him in the morning as she left with the darning for Mrs Povey.

Eloise shouted for the men, and they carried Mr McCreedy to his bed at the back corner of the shed, but he was drenched and feverish and fought them off. They couldn't get him to lie still enough to get him into dry clothes and he shivered and chattered frantically.

Eloise tried to send Martha to fetch the doctor but Martha panicked and couldn't make it out of the shed, a force beyond her control betraying her courage. So Eloise went running, but the doctor was not in his surgery. She went on to find the midwife and by the time they got back, Penelope had hot water boiling and had wrapped Mr McCreedy in blankets. She was trying to make him drink tea, holding the tin cup to his wildly clashing teeth.

The fever passed in a few days, but Mr McCreedy wouldn't or couldn't eat. The doctor came to reset his leg and prescribed Chlordyne for the pain, which the midwife argued upset his stomach and made him push the food away.

"Throw that stuff away and give him chicken soup," the midwife told Penelope, who sent Eloise to the market for a chicken carcass and vegetables.

She made broth. They dunked in chunks of bread and Mr McCreedy sat up and tried to suck it between his teeth.

"He has broken ribs," said the midwife. The doctor disagreed and said he was only bruised, but either way, there was nothing for him but opiates for the pain, and they made him vomit.

When Hemi came home from a week away with the wagons, Mr McCreedy told him to ride to Waipukurau for the girl preacher.

"The girl," he said. "Not her father, that dry old windbag. I want to talk to the girl. Better not hang about, son."

And so while Hemi rode south for Serenity, Eloise and Penelope nursed the wagoner and fed him spoonful by meagre spoonful, and the yard worker Taffy saw that the wagons got loaded and hitched and sent out with contracted riders.

"Put me in my chair!" Mr McCreedy insisted, but Penelope was adamant that he stay in bed, with his leg raised and his torso still. He demanded to see the baby so they brought Winnie downstairs, now toddling, and she climbed over the debris in the yard and pulled on his blankets. Mr McCreedy watched her tripping about and falling, and he cried out with a sharp pain when the child climbed onto his bed, but wouldn't let Martha take her away.

"She's quite something, eh? My little mokopuna. You make sure you take her down to meet Mary in Waipuk. She'll want to see what a little angel that rubbish boy has managed to turn out."

Hemi came back with Serenity late the next afternoon in a buggy. She was wrapped in a travelling rug and covered from the rain. She went immediately in to Mr McCreedy's box bed at the foot of the stairs and the old man waved them all away.

"Take them off to dinner, Hemi!" His voice was weak. He still appeared to shout, but the sound was not big enough to fill his gaping mouth. He took a handful of coins from somewhere under his blankets and threw them towards Hemi. "Here. All of you. Get out. Go to a hotel and don't come back until it is dark. I have things to say and it is not for you to hear. Go on, clear out."

They left him reluctantly. As they left the yard, Eloise looked back at Serenity, who had pulled up a chair close to Mr McCreedy's bedside and was holding the man's hand. His stringy grey hair was falling in tufts and the bald pate beneath was strangely glossy, like a baby's.

"Is he dying?" asked Hemi.

Penelope put her hand on his shoulder. "I don't think he's ready to go yet, Hemi," she told him. "But he will have to slow down a bit."

"I can do more. We can hire another driver and I can run the yard. Stop him getting up and running around like that. He's a crazy man. He's got to rest. I tell him, Mrs Sansonnet. I tell him."

Serenity stayed that night with the family upstairs, sharing Eloise's mattress. Compared to her father's hut in Waipukurau, she said it was luxurious accommodation, and somehow she made them believe that, despite the wind sucking in through the walls and the sharp smell of the horse muck from the stables, God was there, in the cleanly swept room, giving them courage.

She wouldn't tell them what passed between her and Mr McCreedy, but when Eloise suggested he had enjoyed a colourful life and might have a lot to confess, Serenity didn't contradict her.

But she did say that she had seen many dying men, and Mr McCreedy didn't have the look of the dying about him. "I am sure he will recover," she said. "Just keep that doctor away from him."

When Hemi was home Martha stayed downstairs with him, in his little room at the back of the yard. "They are happy?" Serenity asked Eloise. There was little doubt that they were. Martha found happiness in unusual places.

Eloise shrugged. "Of course it's not what we wanted for her," she said. "The whole thing is dreadful. I'm sure not a day goes by that Mother doesn't cry for leaving Cornwall. Our choices have become so limited, Serenity, and to think that of all the family, it's little Martha who is married, and to a Māori who has ended up supporting us all. But yes, she seems happy. She doesn't have fits anymore. She's overwhelmed, sometimes, of course."

"We can all sympathise with that."

"But you know Martha doesn't consider the future, or think about the past particularly. And when she is with Winnie, and Hemi is home, she does seem as happy as she has ever been. But I'm not sure when happiness became the point."

"But Hemi is a good man."

"He is a Māori labourer," said Eloise. "It doesn't make any difference if he is good or not. And no, he's not good. He put a baby in her when she was still almost a child."

"He cares for her."

"Yes," she conceded. "Yes, he cares for her very well."

"Then judge him by his actions now."

Eloise was abashed. "So I should," she said. "He's proved to be more of a gentleman than my father."

Hemi brought Winnie upstairs to say goodnight. He tapped her round little cheeks with his finger as she giggled. It was strange to see a man with a baby on his hip but there was no doubt that Winnie was thriving under his care. When he went back down the stairs, the women could hear him singing to his daughter in his own language.

They took away their warmth with them. Eloise's eyes rested on her mother, tucking up against a stack of boxes on a pallet with a thin mattress, under threadbare, borrowed blankets.

She turned to Serenity. "You and your father came from England to live in a hut and convert the heathen, knowing that you would work among the poor and do good in the world. You have a calling. We didn't come to live like this. Look at my mother! We are so miserable and dependent and doing no good to anyone."

"I don't think that is true. You are looking after Mr McCreedy."

"In payment for us living here."

"It seems more like a family arrangement now." Serenity tucked a blanket around herself and settled her shawl under her head for a pillow. "Would you like to do good?"

"I don't see how I can, now." Eloise plucked at a loose thread on the blanket. "We live in shame. We have lived on the wages of sin and we are all tainted with it. I am sick with it."

"I have asked you before, come with me when I go to Ahuriri. There is a refuge now, where we take the women who are trying to rebuild their lives. They are learning skills, eventually we will place them as domestics on the farms. Will you not help me try to help them?"

But Eloise felt the bile rise in her throat. "How can I? Don't ask me, Serenity. I cannot work with those women. I will come with you to the new immigrants, but don't ask me to befriend prostitutes."

"Their children are innocent, that you must believe."

"Yes, that I do believe."

"Perhaps one day, we might have an orphanage here for mixed race and abandoned immigrant children. There may be money for it, from an unexpected source. Do you think, Eloise, that you and your mother might help me establish an orphanage? It may help you come to terms with what your father has done."

"Yes," Eloise agreed. "I would like to do that. The children could be saved. If it could ever happen."

"I think," said Serenity, changing the subject, "that it is time to baptise the baby. You know my father would be honoured to do it, at the new chapel. Why don't you wait until Mr McCreedy is better and then all come to Waipukurau?"

CHAPTER ELEVEN

It was a beautiful summer's day when they hitched up the wagon and rolled out of Napier. They had on their best clothes, and Hemi had bought them new bonnets and Martha a new dress. This time on the trail, it was Hemi who was driving. Mr McCreedy was in his modified wheeled chair and was lifted onto the back, shouting instructions in a voice that carried far. Mr Duffy was with them, with Mrs Duffy and their two children, sitting opposite the elderly widow Povey, who made faces with the baby. Miss Belle was there, too. Even her grandfather had come out for the day, the first time he had been down country, and they all knew he had come for the adventure every bit as much as for the baptism of the baby.

Billy was up front with Hemi, who let him drive the straight bits so he could feel the horses though the reins, and Billy was happy at his post through the long flat reaches between the hills. The young men laughed and jostled and

Hemi pushed him aside good-naturedly when any actual driving had to be done.

"Give him the reins, go on!" shouted Mr McCreedy from behind. "Let him run us off the road and kill us all! It'll make no difference, we all know a blind man can steer the wagon better than you, boy!"

Down country, they crossed the Tukituki River to where the new church sat, a tiny building, but bright and neat in fresh white paint, a beacon on the road.

Hemi unloaded them, then helped Mr McCreedy down the ramp in his chair and shushed his banter as he wheeled him inside the church. He came back somewhat nervously to collect Martha, and they held a hand each as Winnie toddled into the church for her baptism.

Eloise was with Penelope, standing back to admire the new building when, from the little church office on the side, a man with light gold hair strode out and walked along the path in front of them.

Eloise saw him, and then she saw him.

It was Lars, and he stopped abruptly. They were face to face.

Eloise was instantly overwhelmed.

She had the same intense feeling as when she had run to find him in Napier, crazy to catch a glimpse of him, desperate when she found he had gone. It was as though only seconds had passed and the fury of that moment was no more than a breath away. She was helpless finding him now, on the path before the church, his carefree manner blinked away as they faced each other. He was good and fearless and the heart shape of his face melted her. Her hand tightened on her mother's arm, but her mother was gracious and looked like she used to look in Cornwall, with her open smile and kindly face.

Penelope recognised Lars immediately, and she held Eloise steady as she greeted him and praised him again for the workmanship of the beautiful chair, and told him that they all admire it still, every day. It was like she was meeting a friend in town.

Eloise couldn't understand how Lars could stand there on the path outside the church and talk with her mother;

how he resisted the drag forwards that was so thick between them it melted the air until the grass underfoot blurred with the pressure. She felt a power as if his arms were already around her and his face buried down into her neck. She smelled wood on him, and a sweet sweat that almost made her faint.

Lars replied to Penelope's questions. His family was well and working hard on the farm and no, they hadn't made any more chairs. He got home when he could, but worked now for the railway and was studying at the Engineering Institute.

"My sisters," he told Eloise, finally meeting her eyes, "called their dolls Eloise and Martha and they build houses for them and send them on boats down the river and on adventures into the bush. You are so kind," he said in words, but his eyes ran everywhere over her face and she heard them say, with delight, "You are so lovely."

He hesitated when Penelope asked why he had come to the church. He told them, in a sombre voice, as though at a confessional: he had come to book the reading of the banns for his wedding.

He lifted a piece of folded paper, a flimsy thing in his strong hand. He didn't look proud.

"This is my wedding licence. I have it made, just now."

And he looked past Eloise, past Penelope, his troubled grey eyes unfocused, and he bit his lip, a gesture so utterly defenceless that Eloise could not bear to look at him.

"My mother want I get married for my own good. To stop. Mmm." He made the chopping gesture with his hands parallel, the one she knew so well, which meant so much. "Well. To stop. I am distracted. If I marry I will settle my mind. So she find me a wife, and there."

"She found you a wife?"

"From Wanganui. I meet her father and after we write a letter. I am sure she is very nice."

He finally looked at Eloise. If he saw the tremble on her lip there was nothing he could say.

When words wouldn't come and her mind was in confusion, Eloise knew to fall back on good manners. She'd had no etiquette the night she met Lars on the equator, in her bare feet and nightgown, and there were no rules that prevented him holding her as he lifted her from the horse in Norsewood. But now, here, she found herself in a church courtyard with her mother, and the man she loved was about to marry someone else. There was no doubt of the etiquette required for this situation.

"Congratulations, Mr Nilsen. I do hope you will be happy," she said, and her lips curled into a tight little smile.

She wished she could break and run for the church.

"And you," he asked, almost pleadingly. "You are happy?"

"Yes, thank you. We are all happy." But there were thorns that dragged across her skin and snagged on her heart as she spoke.

"I meet your husband, you know. He is not here?"

"You met my husband?"

"Mr Wainwright. When I come with the chair. I want to bring it because I want to meet him. To know. I hope ... well, no matter now. You are happy."

He had the piece of paper in his hand still. The marriage licence. Eloise couldn't pretend it was of no consequence, and couldn't go on smiling. She turned away to follow the others into the church.

"Goodbye, Lars."

Martha had gone inside but Hemi waited and held the door for Eloise, who stumbled past him. Penelope remained outside. "You go on," her mother said. "I'll be there in a minute."

Once inside the church, with Lars out, there was no wall between them as there should have been. He seemed to have come in with his arms still around her, the way she felt him sometimes when she was sitting in the rocking chair, his love a warm blanket. She could feel his breath on her cheek and was consumed by his voice inside her head – come back, he said over and over, come back, come back. It was unbearable.

She folded into the nearest pew and wrapped her arms around herself, rocking slightly, the way Martha did sometimes, to block out the world.

From the front of the small church she heard the minister's piping voice greeting his congregation.

Eventually, she opened her eyes and looked around her. She was surprised to see there was a large community inside. Gathered in the pews were Māori people, men, women and children, one large family perhaps. They were dressed formally in Sunday best. Some of the women wore big decorative hats and some had feathers poked into their hair. It was a strange, mixed congregation. Eloise recognised Mary, who had a collar of pale lace on a blue shiny dress, as if it was a wedding she had come to, and she the bride. Perhaps these people were Hemi's family. Eloise had never thought about his Māori family. It never occurred to her that he would invite them to the christening or that they would be churchgoers, and part of this congregation. She found it extraordinary that she had never asked him about his mother's family, never given him the simple courtesy of asking the question: who are your people?

Martha was at the front, holding the baby, the centre of attention. She blinked frantically and shrunk from the garden of faces, all staring at her. Everything was new and erratic and Eloise was pained to see the naivety of her sister exposed so blatantly.

But Hemi was with her and he spoke quickly to his people in Māori, all the time with his hand on Martha, rubbing her arm gently, rubbing her back. She lowered her head to hide in the baby's arms but after a moment, coaxed by Hemi, she straightened back up and was in control. There was an audible sigh of relief from the congregation. They were on her side, all these people, helping her through.

Eloise heard nothing of Mr Wix's sermon. She only heard Lars.

I hope you are happy. I am happy. We are all happy.

I am not happy, Lars. The last time I was truly happy was when you had your arms around me. Are you happy? Why is your voice in my head if you are happy? Why?

Penelope joined her in the pew. She picked up her hand and squeezed it. Eloise realised she was crying.

Serenity saw them there and came back. She asked no questions, but slipped in to sit on the other side so the two women held Eloise between them.

When they were all settled and ready, Mr Wix called Winnie forwards, and the baby was duly baptised and welcomed into the church. A tattooed, older Māori man stood and spoke in a musical language, a song of calling and reply. It sounded like a language of the outdoors, one that flowed in the trees and rivers. Eloise found the sound incredibly soothing. The words, whatever they meant, were about love.

After the Baptism service was over, the Māori man asked Serenity to lead them in prayers. They had come a long way, and they wanted to hear the girl preacher.

Eloise put her hand on her friend's sleeve.

"Serenity," she said quietly. "Can you talk about love? Please?"

"Oh, my dear." She took her friend's hand in hers, and brushed away her tears with the other. "Yes. I can talk about love. Though I think you probably know more about love than I will ever know."

She went to the front, and her father stepped aside for her. There was a shuffling in the seats as they all sat straighter and gave their full attention forwards. Winnie was awake in her father's arms, looking out into the faces of her family, throwing her generous smile around.

Serenity was calm and clear and they fell under the spell of her voice.

If I speak in the tongues of men or of angels, but do not have love, I am only a resounding gong or a clanging cymbal. If I have the gift of prophecy and can fathom all mysteries and all knowledge, and if I have a faith that can move mountains, but do not have love, I am nothing. If I give all I possess to the poor and give over my body to hardship that I may boast, but do not have love, I gain nothing.

Love is patient, love is kind. It does not envy, it does not boast, it is not proud. It does not dishonour others, it is not self-seeking, it is not easily angered, it keeps no record of wrongs. Love does not delight in evil but rejoices with the truth. It always protects, always trusts, always hopes, always preserves.

They sat enraptured in the close and stuffy chapel. Serenity's words ran along the walls and high ceiling and settled on them as they perched on the wooden pews, hot and still. The bright light of the southern hemisphere bounced off sun-drenched plains and scattered across the country, streaming through the coloured window behind the girl. She spoke words they all knew and recognised but she had a magic that turned them around so they were more than words repeated from a liturgy. Her words held a message unique to each of them, so they breathed them in and remembered them and the feeling stayed with them long after they had gone back to their everyday lives.

***

When the prayers were over they shook themselves awake. The room was stifling. Serenity led them out and they rose as one and headed for the doors, flowing out into the fresh air all together like starlings from a tree, streaming away from the hall and down the path in formation, wing-tip apart.

Eloise was on the edge and someone stepped in alongside her.

It was Lars, who had waited for her. The white piece of paper was nowhere in sight. He joined on her wing, hovering tentatively, and for a few steps they were side by side with the swarm.

They floated over the ground, through the warm air, in a meadow of wildflowers.

And then he veered off, and as he turned he held his hand out behind him.

Of course she took it, and they broke away from the flock and went over the field together, across the rough grass, and down to the river where they settled on wide flat stones to talk about what was to be done. They were as familiar with each other as love.

ACKNOWLEDGEMENTS

To my Larsen family, who emigrated from Norway all those years ago, thank you for your courage.

I love all the support and encouragement I get from my family: Paul, David, Annie and Guy and the wider whanau. You're the best.

Thanks to my readers: Cheryl Sucher, Viv Aitken, Gareth Ward and especially Fleur Beale who pulled the story together; and, as always, to Mandy Hager for inspiration and craft. Thanks Andy for the peaceful Paihia residence where I edited.

I'd like to acknowledge Tessa Duder for decades of inspiration and the Storylines Award that made publication possible; and thanks to the team at Walker Books for your patience and care.